# SANDRA GLOVER

Sandra Glover took a History degree at the University of Lancaster before becoming a teacher. She now divides her time between writing and working with children on creative writing projects. She has published twelve books and has been shortlisted for several awards including: the Lancashire Children's Book of the Year Award, the South Lanarkshire Children's Book Award and the Leicester Book Award. She is best known for her hard-hitting teenage novels, such as *The Girl Who Knew* and *Face to Face*.

Sandra lives in Cumbria with her family and her dogs, Muppet and Morse.

USBORNE THRILLERS

Terry Deary
*The Boy Who Haunted Himself*

Ann Evans
*The Beast*

Malcolm Rose
*The Tortured Wood*

Paul Stewart
*The Curse of Magoria*

# Demon's Rock

## SANDRA GLOVER

USBORNE

For my daughter, Katrina

———————————

First published in 2004 by Usborne Publishing Ltd., Usborne House,
83-85 Saffron Hill, London EC1N 8RT, England. www.usborne.com

A CIP catalogue record for this book is available from the British Library.

ISBN  0 7460 6037 8  Printed in Great Britain.

# Chapter One

I'm fairly sure that, until a few months ago, we were a completely normal family. Very ordinary. In fact, ordinary to the point of dullness most of the time. Dad's an accountant and you don't get much duller than that. Mum's a veterinary nurse. Not really important except it explains why we live in the country on the edge of the moors...so that the ever-increasing army of limping dogs, half-blind cats, geriatric goats and other strays she brings home have plenty of space to exercise.

So, apart from Mum's peculiar pets, they were Mr. and Mrs. Extremely Average with their two children: a boy aged twelve (that's me) and a girl, aged ten (my sister, Mona). She's not really called that. Her name's Anna-Mae, but I re-christened her Mona because that's what she was always doing. Moaning. Usually about me.

"Go away," she'd wail. "Quit bugging me!"

Which is how I came to be known as Bug. Almost everyone calls me that now. Parents, friends, neighbours, the lot. Only my teachers ever call me Benjamin.

Anyway, we were bickering away quite normally on a dreary Friday night at the start of October half-term, little knowing that our life was about to be thrown into total chaos.

We'd just finished dinner. Mum and Dad were poring over their latest bank statement. See what I mean about dull? And Mona and me were standing by the dishwasher, arguing about whose turn it was to stack it.

"I did it last night."

"No, you didn't!"

"Yes, I did."

Honestly, it was like the Christmas panto come early. Not very imaginative, as far as arguments go. But then neither of us has what you'd call a good imagination. We never really played fantasy games, even when we were younger. We're both more practical types. Which is important.

We're totally sane, too. Though you might not believe it once you've heard my story. But everything I'm going to tell you is true, I promise. However unlikely, however bizarre it seems and whatever my parents might say, my story is true.

It all started with the shout from outside. A really loud, high-pitched, terrifying scream, which drowned out our bickering.

"Mum!" it squealed. "Mum, help me! Help me! What's happening?"

Seconds later the back door burst open, letting in a blast of cold air and a swirl of damp leaves that settled on the kitchen floor.

We all looked and there was this lad standing in the open doorway, breathing so heavily it sounded like a dog panting. The lad was white. Not just as in white-skinned but completely, ghostly, ghastly white.

His short, brown hair was stuck up in little spikes, like he'd had some terrible shock. Or maybe he'd just been running his hands through it while it was wet. Very wet. Like the rest of him. So wet that the funny knitted sweater he was wearing was all sort of misshapen, dripping down over seriously naff grey trousers.

His lack of fashion sense intrigued me for about ten seconds until he screamed again. Which sort of distracted me a bit. Not least because Mona screamed in response. Mum and Dad leaped up. The dogs whimpered and scurried under the table while the two cats that had been lying, peacefully, on the floor, hurled themselves on top of the fridge-freezer, backs arched, tails fluffed up.

And the boy...well, he seemed to somehow move forwards and backwards at the same time, still screaming and waving his arms around, as if he didn't quite know what to do.

The wind slamming the door shut behind him made the decision for him, I guess. He pressed his back flat against it, arms outstretched like a squashed cartoon character. Staring at us with wide blue eyes as if we were three-headed space monsters or something.

Somewhere, somehow, in all the noise and chaos, his screams had started to form into words.

"Who are you? What are you doing here? Stop them! Stop them! What have they done to me? I want my mum. Where is she? What have you done with her?"

I'm not sure I've got his words in the right order, but it doesn't really matter. Whatever order they were in, they didn't make much sense. Not least because they were spoken so rapidly, it was like being under fire from a hail of bullets, which made me want to dive under the table with the dogs.

"Where's my dad? And Peter? Who are you? Why are you in my house?" he rattled on.

A clue at last! The boy had got confused. Wandered into our house, instead of his own. Only he wasn't local, I was sure. Our village is tiny, even if you count the new houses. Everyone more or less knows everyone else. And I definitely hadn't seen him before. New to the area, then? Visiting a relative?

I suppose the same sort of confused thoughts were going through my parents' heads and Mona's. Because, unusually for us, we were all completely silent for a moment.

It was Mum who spoke first.

"Are you all right?" she asked the boy.

Daft question or what? It was obvious that he was anything *but* all right.

"Have you had an accident?" Mum went on.

All the time the boy was still gibbering. Not attempting to answer the questions at all. Not even communicating with us. More talking to himself.

"Where am I? What's happened? What have they done? Where's my mum? I want my mum."

He started frantically rubbing his eyes and pinching his arms, as if he expected to wake up any minute and break free of whatever nightmare he thought he was in.

Us! We were his nightmare. And when we refused to disappear, he started howling and bashing his head against the door. Really heavy thuds.

Mum tried to stop him, hold him, comfort him, like she does with all her distressed creatures, but no animal could have fought her off as fiercely as he did. Arms and legs thrashing around, teeth bared like a werewolf with rabies.

We heard the sharp crack as one of his heavy shoes made contact with Mum's shin. She backed off, limping. Mona started crying and Dad whispered that he was going to call the police. Well, what else are you supposed to do when some crazy kid bursts in and starts attacking you in your own home?

I don't know whether the boy heard what Dad said, but he suddenly whirled round, grabbed the door handle and tried to make his escape.

That handle's a bit stiff at the best of times and, as he tried to wrestle with it, all strength seemed to drain from him and he collapsed. Slumped on the floor, he lay so still I really thought he was dead.

Can you imagine what that's like? One

minute you're pottering around arguing about dishwashers and the next you've got a dead body on your kitchen floor!

For a split second, none of us moved. We all stood there rigid with shock until he groaned slightly, prompting Mum to rush forward and lift him up. Not dead, then. But ill enough for Dad to change his emergency call from police to police and ambulance.

"Lavelle," he said. "Mr. and Mrs. Lavelle. Moor Lane Farm."

It's not a farm. Hasn't been for twenty years or more. Not since old farmer whatever-he-was-called died and most of the land was sold off for building development. But the house still keeps the name, a small field and a couple of outbuildings where Mum's four-legged friends live.

"That's right," Dad was saying. "A boy. Looks like he's had some sort of accident. He's rambling. Delirious. No. I've no idea. Never seen him before."

It was over half an hour before the cops and ambulance turned up. Not exactly the rapid-response team. Good job the boy wasn't breathing his last, as I'd feared, but had only fainted.

Mum had managed to lie him on the settee before he started to come round. We all stood back as his eyes fluttered open, but we needn't have worried.

Not about violence, anyway. All the fight, all the aggression, had gone. He wasn't even shouting any more. He just lay there pale and trembling slightly. His eyes were open but unseeing, like he was in total shock.

We wondered whether we should do anything. Try to give him food or drink. Talk to him or just leave him alone.

In the end, Dad covered him with a blanket and Mum sat beside him, forcing sips of water between his frozen lips. The water seemed to revive him and he started to talk again. Muttering to himself. The same sort of mad rambling.

"Where am I? What's happened? Where's Daddy? My head hurts. And my eyes. Where's Peter? What have they done to me?"

We thought he might flip again when the cops and paramedics turned up, but he barely seemed to notice at first. Carried on muttering while Dad told the cops what little we knew.

A lady officer took Mum's place on the settee after a paramedic had said that it was okay to ask the boy a few questions. The rest of us stood around, not wanting to interfere, but curious about what the boy might say.

The lady cop was good. Obviously trained to deal with trauma victims. Some quiet words of reassurance first. Then the questions.

"Can you tell me your name?" she asked.

Somehow, I hadn't expected the boy to answer. But whatever memory loss or shock he'd suffered, he clearly knew who he was.

"Joe," he said. "Joe Hadley."

The words weren't screamed or muttered either. They were spoken clearly, as if he were pleased that someone had asked him a nice, normal question. Something he could answer. Something he could deal with.

"And your address?"

"Moor Lane Farm," he began.

The male cop looked down at the notes he'd been scribbling and then at us. Dad shook his head.

"You live at Moor Lane Farm?" the lady officer repeated. "You mean, you *think* you live here."

"I do!" Joe said, agitation flooding into his voice again. "Only it's wrong. It's different. It's changed. When I came back, *they* were here. Those funny people."

Funny people? Did he mean us? He obviously did.

"You say they were here when you got back," said the lady, while I wondered what exactly was supposed to be odd about us. "Do you know how long you'd been away?"

"A couple of hours," said Joe, confidently. "Only a couple of hours."

"We've lived here almost three years," Dad whispered, shaking his head again. "And we've never seen him before."

"It's not just them," said Joe, distracted and confused again. "It's all changed. Everything's changed. The village. The fields. The fields have gone! There are houses. Everything's changed. All our furniture's gone. What's happening? What's happening to me?"

He'd turned even paler than he'd been before, if that was possible, and this crazy idea leaped into my head that he was some sort of ghost. Only ghosts don't kick and leave bruises on people's shins, do they? They're not solid. You can't touch them, can you?

"When you went out, when you left the house...an hour or two ago," said the lady, "where did you go?"

"Out on the moors," said Joe. "With Bobby."

We all started head-shaking. None of us had heard of anyone called Bobby, any more than we knew Joe Hadley.

"And Bobby is?"

"My pony," said the boy.

"So you went riding on the moors...?"

"It was them!" he yelled, sitting bolt upright as though someone had suddenly pulled a string. "It was them. It must have been them! They did this."

"The Lavelles?" said the lady. "You think the Lavelles have...?"

"No, not them!" said Joe. "Those things. Up on the moor. The elves."

I couldn't help it. I burst out laughing. Stopped myself as everyone turned to look at me.

"Those red things," said Joe, looking really scared. "Red things in the flames. Elves. Goblins. Imps. Devils. I don't know. I mean, I don't believe in that sort of stuff..."

Well, that was one bit of good news, anyway.

"But I saw them. I saw them. They tried to grab me. After the explosion. I ran off. Came home. It's some sort of spell, isn't it? They did it, didn't they? They've made me see things. Things that aren't really here."

Fantastic, I thought. Now we were figments of his imagination caused by little red men casting spells.

Joe prodded at the police officer, as if trying to test how real she was. Prodding harder and harder in frustration until she gently grabbed his hand. At the same time she glanced at the paramedics. It was obviously time to take poor Joe, or whoever he was, to the hospital. Anyone who sat there ranting on about imps and elves clearly wasn't too well.

"We'll need to run some checks," the lady told the male officer. "See if we can trace a family by the name of Hadley. Let me just see if I can get a little more information."

She smiled at Joe.

"All right," she said. "Just a few more questions. How old are you?"

"Eleven."

"And can you tell me your date of birth?"

Familiar ground again. I could tell by the look on his face that he could answer that one, too.

"The fourth of August," he began, confidently. "1952."

# Chapter Two

**S**adly, I haven't inherited my dad's passion for maths. But you don't need to be a genius to know that someone born in 1952 would be a touch older than 11, do you? Not only was it decades before I was born, it was also a good few years before either Mum or Dad had launched themselves into the world.

"Do you mean 1992, perhaps?" the police lady asked.

"Don't be daft!" said Joe and he sort of smiled. A shy little grin which only lasted a second. But it was there. As though he genuinely found her idea funny.

One reason Joe's smile didn't last was that the

paramedics had suggested it might be time to get him to hospital. An idea Joe wasn't keen on. He jumped up, hurled himself off the settee and started racing round the room, screaming again.

"I'm not going! I'm not going with you! I'm staying here. This is my house. I want my mum."

Not finding her, he threw himself at the nearest substitute, I guess. Grabbing hold of *my* mum, wrapping his arms round her so tightly that I wasn't sure whether he was trying to hug her or kill her.

Mum had no such doubts. Joe might not have had four legs, fins or scales but he was a creature in need and Mum couldn't resist him. She held on to him, stroking his hair as he sobbed in her arms.

"I don't suppose he could stay...?"

The police and paramedics shook their heads and, in the end, Mum had to accept it. People were different to animals. You couldn't just pick them up off the street, or even off your own kitchen floor and take them in. There are rules, regulations, forms and procedures.

Joe had to go to hospital and that was that. No matter that he had to be carried out kicking and screaming, still raving on about elves, explosions and the funny people who'd taken over his home.

"Let us know," Mum said as they left. "We'd like

to know how he gets on. If you trace his family and everything."

Her voice was already cracking and the minute they left she burst into tears. She's a real softie, my mum. I've seen her get upset when she's accidentally drowned a spider in the sink, so none of us was really surprised that she was howling over the poor mad kid who'd turned up on our doorstep.

"He'll be best off at the hospital," Dad said. "He's obviously had some sort of accident, hasn't he? Perhaps fell off his pony, banged his head? I mean he wasn't wearing a riding hat or anything."

"Wasn't wearing any sort of riding gear," I said. "So maybe there never was a pony. Maybe he imagined it along with the elves."

"It's odd though, isn't it?" said Mona.

"Oh, no," I said. "Happens all the time. Eleven-year-old boys who were born in 1952, turning up, claiming to live in your house."

"Shut it, Bug. I was thinking."

"First time for everything."

"I mean, maybe he really did live here...once."

"Can't have done," said Dad. "We've been here for three years. The people before us were called Bromley not Hadley and they'd been here for fifteen years or more. Before that it was old farmer what's-his-name. Can't remember his surname but it definitely wasn't Hadley."

"It's still odd," said Mona, stating the mind-numbingly obvious again. "Like he was a ghost or something, wandering about in the wrong time. I mean, those clothes..."

"Ghost!" I said. "Don't be pathetic."

Okay, I know I'd thought of the ghost theory too but I wasn't going to admit it, was I?

"It's not pathetic," said Mona. "Think about it. If he's eleven and if he was really born in 1952—"

"He wasn't!" I interrupted. "He couldn't have been, could he?"

"Okay," said Mona. "But he *thinks* he was. So this would be 1963 to him, wouldn't it? He kept saying that everything was different, didn't he? I mean who lived here in the sixties?"

"No idea," said Dad.

"The sixties! Oh, I get it! You think Joe's come in a time machine, right? Made by his mad scientist uncle back in 1963. It's obvious isn't it? Why didn't I think of that?"

"Shut it, Bug. You always twist what I'm trying to say."

"Talking of time," said Dad, vacantly. "I think it's time you two were getting ready for bed."

I looked at the kitchen clock, ready to make my usual protest.

*6:35.*

That couldn't be right. I checked my watch.

*18:34.*

Strange. Dad checked his. Same sort of time. Mona checked. Mum checked. We couldn't find a clock or watch in the house that didn't insist it was around half past six. About the time Joe had turned up!

"Bit of a coincidence," said Dad. "What is he? Some sort of Uri Geller?"

I wasn't sure what a Uri Geller was but Mum explained that he was a conjuror who claimed to have genuine paranormal powers to stop and start watches, bend spoons and stuff just by looking at them.

As far as I knew, none of our spoons was bent and Dad finally tracked down the right time on his mobile. Whatever had stopped all the other clocks clearly hadn't got to the phone.

"Almost half past nine," Dad announced, triumphantly, as he started to reset all the clocks. "Definitely time for you two to make a move."

"Bug hasn't done the dishwasher yet," moaned Mona.

"It's your turn."

"No, it isn't."

"Oh, yes, it is."

And there we were, back to normal. Or so I thought. Until the phone rang in the middle of the night.

It was the ringing that woke us but it was Mum's shrieks that brought us out of our bedrooms and crashing downstairs.

"Oh, no!" Mum yelled down the phone. "Haven't they got any security, or what? Wasn't anyone watching him? I mean, they must have known there was a risk. Yes. Yes. I know. I'm sorry. Thanks for letting us know. No, he hasn't come back here. Yes, I will. Of course. Bye."

She turned. Saw the three of us standing, staring expectantly.

"He's disappeared," she said. "Joe's disappeared from the hospital. The police want us to let them know if he comes back here."

I blinked sleepily at the clock. It was working. Seven minutes past three. And, selfish as it might seem, I was more concerned about my disturbed sleep than the thought of the mad kid wandering about in the middle of the night in the rain.

Dad and Mona followed me upstairs and I guess we all thought that would be the end of the matter.

But no! When I staggered down for breakfast on Saturday morning, there was Joe! Sitting with Mum. Eating toast. Drinking hot chocolate. Both of them damp and shivery.

Joe's clothes were hanging to dry and I noticed that he was wearing a blue sweatshirt and jeans. Mona's sweatshirt, my jeans! Both too big for him.

I've no idea at what point during the night he turned up or how he got back to us. I mean, that hospital's miles away. So I wouldn't be surprised if Mum had gone out in the car looking for him.

But she never admitted to anything at the time and if I ask her now... Well, I know there'd be no point now.

One thing was for sure. She hadn't done as instructed. She hadn't phoned the police. Almost snapped Dad's head off later when he suggested it.

"I will," she said. "Soon. I'm not stupid, you know."

It's funny, isn't it? The things you do, the things you feel in unusual circumstances. I mean, I didn't feel sorry for Joe or worried about him. Not then. Not on that Saturday morning. I felt jealous. Jealous of all the fuss Mum was giving him. I never felt jealous of the bunnies or bent-beaked budgies but Joe was different. He was a boy. Like me. And he was taking my place!

Mona felt the same. Started playing up. Whingeing that he was dressed in her best sweatshirt. That she'd planned on wearing it that morning.

"You've got other sweatshirts," Mum snapped. "Put one of those on."

Mum clearly wasn't herself. Barking orders at Dad and us. Feed the animals. Go and do the shopping. Don't forget to empty the dishwasher.

Then it was back to soft, sympathetic mode. Back to Joe. Who ignored her for a while and stared, instead, at the dishwasher.

"You put plates in a machine," he muttered to himself. "To wash them! And they don't get broken?"

"He's like this about everything," Mum whispered. "You should have seen him with the microwave when I warmed the milk. It was like he'd never seen one before."

Yeah, right, I thought. Who did he think he was kidding? And just who the heck was he? Even worse, what was he doing to my mum? It was like he'd completely taken her over.

Dad said that it was nothing sinister.

"You know your mum," he said, as we drove to the shops. "Can't resist a sad case, can she? I'm just worried about what the police will say, though. When they realize he's been here half the morning!"

But when we got back, it quickly became clear that Mum hadn't even phoned the police...or the hospital!

I found myself glancing at the clock when I came in. Maybe the movement had caught my eye. The movement of the hands whirring round and round, in a way they shouldn't. My digital watch was flashing too. Random numbers popping up on the display.

Coincidence? A bit unlikely. But then the possibility of it having something to do with Joe was just a touch unlikely too. Or so I thought at the time.

He seemed quite calm when we got back. They'd moved on from hot chocolate and were now sipping tea.

"I'll make my own then, shall I?" I said when we'd finished unpacking the shopping.

Mum barely looked up.

"Go on, Joe," she said. "What happened after you had the argument with your dad?"

"He hit me," said Joe. "Across the head."

A blow on the head! Well, that could explain a lot!

"Not hard," said Joe. "But it made me angry. Because it wasn't me that had left the gate open at all. It was our Peter. But Dad never blames Peter for anything. He says he's only little. Only five. He doesn't know any different. So it's up to me to watch him. But I don't think that's fair!"

Joe was starting to sound just like my sister! I winked at Mona, drawing attention to the similarity and she stuck her tongue out at me.

"I just wanted to get away for a bit," said Joe. "Not for ever. I wasn't running away or nothing. I wasn't. I just jumped on Bobby and rode off."

So that might explain why he didn't have a riding hat or anything. If there ever was a pony. If anything he was saying were true.

None of us knew what Mum and Joe had been talking about all morning, but she'd obviously got his trust. He was chatting away now. Ignoring us. His eyes fixed on Mum.

"I rode onto the moors. I always do," he said. "I never get lost or anything. And I always come back before dark. But it happened so sudden."

"What did?" said Mum.

"The storm," Joe said. "No rain or anything but I heard thunder and these clouds came down. Really low, black clouds."

"I don't like this," Dad whispered. "It just doesn't sound true. There hasn't been a storm or anything. Not recently. I reckon he's spinning your mum a story.

And she's falling for it. Look at her."

I looked at Mum. Her eyes fixed on Joe. I could see why Dad was worried. I was worried! But there was no real reason why Joe's story shouldn't be true...in a way. The weather can change on the moors. Really suddenly. It can be quite different up there to back here. Dad knows that. It's the reason Mona and me aren't allowed to go out on the moors on our own. Well, that and stranger danger.

"I turned back," said Joe. "But I was already a long way out and the clouds were so low I could barely tell where I was. It was dark. Darker than I'd ever seen it. Until the lightning came. Streaks at first. Dozens of them. One after another. Then sheets."

Sheet lightning! That couldn't be right. We'd have surely noticed if there'd been a storm that close.

"Everything was lit up," said Joe, breathlessly. "And I saw the rock. Demon's Rock."

Mona and I looked at each other. We knew Demon's Rock. Everyone round here does. It's a local landmark. Great, huge thing, that's supposed to be in the shape of a crouching demon, standing among a group of smaller rocks. The jagged main section is the hunched back. The lumpy bit is the head. Not that it looks anything like a head, of course.

"Ah," say the dafter locals. "That's because the

head's covered by the demon's arm. If you look carefully you can make out the bulge of a crooked nose and the curve of huge, sneering lips."

Well, I'd looked a dozen times and all I could ever see was a massive lump of rock. Okay, so if you really used your imagination you might just believe that the two sharp peaks look a bit like misshapen horns. But, like I said, I've never had much of an imagination, so it didn't look anything like a demon to me. And I'd certainly never believed any of the stories about it. How it got its name and all the weird things that are supposed to have happened up there over the years.

Now, of course, I know differently. I know things about that rock I'd much rather not know. But that day, when Joe was telling us his crazy story, it was just a rock.

"I recognized it," Joe was saying. "I knew I was nearly home."

"Then what happened?" said Mum.

"You won't believe me," said Joe.

"Try," said Mum. "Just tell me."

"The rock changed," he said. "Started to burn."

"Burn?" said Mum.

"All sort of orange and bright," said Joe. "Swirling flames and sparks like fireworks exploding."

He was right. I didn't believe him. If he'd said a tree or something, you'd think it had been struck by lightning. But not a rock, for goodness' sake. I mean rocks just don't catch fire, do they?

"Bobby reared up," Joe said. "I slid off. I hadn't bothered with a saddle or anything and I just slid off."

So, another possible knock on the head? Or had the lightning actually struck him? Fried his brains? It must have been something like that, I thought. Because, if what he'd said so far sounded a bit strange, what followed was completely, utterly crazy. Absolutely A1-class sort of crazy.

# Chapter Three

"The swirls of fire got bigger," said Joe. "I scrambled up. Tried to run. But I got caught by the flames."

Well, that sort of proved it was rubbish, didn't it? Okay, he looked pretty shaken but there wasn't a mark on him. Certainly no burns. Not so much as a scorched eyelash.

"I could feel the heat," he said, as if answering my thoughts. "But the flames didn't burn me."

Ah, I thought, non-burning flames. Well, that explained it!

"It was like they were all around," he said, clearly

drifting off into some other reality. "Even inside me. But not really touching me. I didn't know where I was. I didn't know what was happening. I screamed and they tried to grab me."

"Who did?" I said, as Mum glared at me.

I knew what he was going to say but I couldn't help testing him to see if he'd stick to his stupid story.

"Those red things," he said. "Coming out of the fire. Long, red arms, trying to grab me! I think they touched me but I pulled away. Threw myself forward, out of the flames onto the ground again. When I stood up, the flames and the lightning had gone. It was dark again. But I was sure they were still there. In the blackness. Reaching out for me. So I ran. Just ran. Towards home. Over the moor, across the fields. Only the fields weren't there any more. Where they were supposed to be. It was houses. All houses. I thought I'd come out on the wrong side of the moor but then I saw the church tower. Followed it. Found my house."

"*Our* house," said Mona.

Mum looked as though she was about to growl at her. Tell her to be quiet. But suddenly there was a rattling sound and our eyes were all drawn to the Welsh dresser where Mum keeps her best plates and mugs.

Plates and mugs that were now jiggling around,

like there was some sort of earth tremor going on. It only lasted a fraction of a second, as tremors in this country do, but it was enough to jolt two of the plates out of position and send them crashing down, smashing into fragments on the kitchen floor. Two of Mum's special plates. The ones she'd brought back from Italy.

It was a bit freaky and Mum was clearly upset about her plates. But she didn't have time to dwell on it because Joe went positively crazy. Running round in circles, treading on the broken plates, crying for his mum and dad. Nothing seemed to calm him and eventually we all gave up, leaving Mum to it.

Dad took matters into his own hands, phoning the police, telling them Joe was back with us. They promised to come round right away. They didn't. In fact they still hadn't turned up by one o'clock when we started scavenging for lunch.

Mum was still talking to Joe, who, mercifully, seemed to have calmed down again. Dad made some eggs on toast. He presented some to Joe just as he was asking one of his weird questions.

"It's not true, is it?" Joe said, nibbling a bit of toast. "What they told me at the hospital? About the date."

"What did they tell you, Joe?" Mum asked.

Joe rattled off the date, stressing the year.

"It can't be true, can it?" he said, all wide-eyed and shaking. "It can't be the twenty-first century, can it? It can't be. Why did they tell me that? Why are they trying to frighten me? What are they trying to do?"

We all looked at each other. Wondering what to do. Tell him it was true? Risk him kicking off again?

"So what year do you think it is, then?" said motor-mouth Mona.

We knew the answer, of course. Even before he said it.

"1963. It should be 1963."

He looked at us, and then looked round the kitchen as he spoke.

"But it doesn't look right," he admitted.

Okay, I thought, as he left his lunch, got up, opened the freezer and stuck his hand inside. What have we got? A boy from 1963, goes out on the moor, has a close encounter with a burning rock and/or a few elves and lands up forty-odd years in the future.

*Or*, perfectly normal twenty-first century boy gets a bump on the head and thinks he's from some other time.

*Or*, completely crazy boy, on the run from some sort of trouble perhaps, decides to pull some weird trick on us.

Discounting the first possibility, I was still

debating between the other two when Joe came and sat down again, bringing with him a pack of oven chips, which he proceeded to open and examine.

Did they have freezers back in 1963? Was he familiar with oven chips? I guessed not by the way he was snapping and dissecting them.

But then, why was I even thinking in this way? He wasn't really from 1963, was he? He couldn't be.

"Do you know who the Prime Minister is, Joe?" Dad said, rescuing and replacing the chips.

Clever, eh? Trust Dad to come up with a devious question.

"Er," said Joe, screwing up his forehead. "Er...no."

Brilliant! We'd caught him out, first try! If he'd known anything at all about the sixties, he'd have known who was running the country, wouldn't he?

"No need to smirk, Bug," said Mum, not quite catching on to what Dad was playing at. "Loads of kids don't know the name of the Prime Minister."

"Okay," said Dad. "Forget politics. What about football? I bet you like football, don't you?"

Joe nodded.

"Who's your favourite player, then?" I asked.

"Bobby Charlton," he answered, excitedly. "He's the best, he is! That's who my pony's named after. We called him Bobby because he used to kick a lot. Before I trained him."

Well, I'd heard of Bobby Charlton. I mean what fan hasn't? Man United. Not to mention England's glory days that all the commentators harp on about when we're losing fifteen-nil to Lapland or whoever.

"Yeah," I said. "1966 World Cup victory and all that but..."

"Do you think so?" said Joe, suddenly animated. "Do you think we'll win the Cup in '66?"

"I think you could safely bet on it, yeah," I said, giving him one of my withering looks. "Germany 2, England 4, thanks to Geoff Hurst's hat-trick. Pretty neat, but I don't reckon any of those old players were as good as David Beckham."

"Who?" he said. "I don't think I know him."

Didn't know Beckham! There are kids in the Gobi Desert and the Arctic Circle who've heard of Beckham. Sports haters, who can't even tell you what shape a football is, have heard of David Beckham.

So either Joe was very devious or he had a nasty case of amnesia. But it wasn't amnesia, was it? He hadn't lost his memory exactly. He knew his name. He knew Demon's Rock. He knew Bobby Charlton. But whatever memory function he had, it sure worked differently to ours.

During the rest of lunch we carried on with the questions. At least me, Mona and Dad did, while Mum glared at us, angry that we should try to trick her funny little friend.

We discovered loads of common ground. Joe, it seemed, liked The Beatles. Well, so do my parents. Dad's got a CD of their greatest hits that he insists on playing at full volume in the car. But Joe claimed not to know most of their songs. Thought Dad was making it up! In Joe's muddled mind The Beatles were a really new group. The latest thing!

It was the same with TV. Sure, Joe liked watching it but claimed not to know any of the celebrities or programmes we talked about. Said he liked a programme about a talking horse and some cop programme that certainly wasn't *The Bill*. Things I'd never heard of but Mum and Dad nodded as though they might have done.

It was all pretty obvious stuff, I guess. I mean if, for some weird reason, you wanted to pretend to be from 1963, it would be easy enough to look it all up, wouldn't it? Who the stars of the day were and what was showing on TV?

But while I became more and more convinced that Joe was some sort of confidence trickster, trying to pull off some crazy hoax, Joe clearly thought the tricks were all on our side.

As we talked and tried to eat, he kept getting up, walking about, poking and prodding at things, giving us funny looks. Sometimes asking questions. Sometimes answering ours. Sometimes just muttering to himself.

"What's happened to all our stuff? How have you done this? Why have you changed everything? Who are you?"

He kept looking in cupboards and drawers. Examining perfectly ordinary things like knives and forks. As if hoping, expecting, to find something familiar.

"These aren't ours," he'd murmur in disappointment. "It's all gone. Everything's gone. Everything!"

He started getting more agitated. Flicking the kitchen lights on and off. Or so I thought at first. But no. When I looked up, he was grubbing around in a cupboard, taking out packets of noodles. Nowhere near the light switch at all.

Yet still the strip light flashed.

"Tube must be going," said Dad. "Or the activator thing."

Well, that was the logical explanation, sure. And it seemed reasonable enough at the time. Before all the other freaky stuff started to happen.

But I shouldn't get on to that yet. I need to try and tell it how it happened. In the right order. And I suppose the next important event was when the cops turned up, in the afternoon.

Mum had asked me and Mona to look after Joe for a while. Talk to him. Show him our rooms.

"Just be normal with him," she said. "So he feels more relaxed and settled. Just accept him, okay? Stop harassing him with questions."

Not as easy as it sounded. It's pretty hard to be normal around a complete nutter. Someone who squeals when you turn on the TV.

"The pictures! They come on right away! They're not black and white! They're like real life! That's amazing."

Someone who keeps bashing the buttons on the remote, leaping up and down in excitement as the channels and volume change. Someone who yelps at you to play one of those funny little records again. Meaning your CDs. Someone who paws and claws at everything, muttering and shrieking to himself.

"All these things! Where have they come from? What's going on? It's some sort of trick, isn't it?"

He went completely wild in my bedroom. Pinching his arms. Screwing his eyes up tight, then opening them again. Over and over. Like he was having a bad dream. Insisting it was *his* room and asking what I'd done with his Meccano and where I'd hidden his clothes and his train set.

It was exhausting. Completely, utterly exhausting. I was glad when a car, drawing up outside, distracted him. Except that when he looked out of the bedroom window and saw it was the cops, he promptly dived under my bed!

Mona and I shrugged and decided to leave him cowering under the bed while we went to check out the latest news from the police. Though we soon wished we hadn't bothered.

There were two cops in the lounge when we got downstairs. PC Cooper, who was the bloke from the previous day. And another, obviously more senior cop, a detective called Barrington.

"Sorry we're a bit late," said Barrington. "I've been trying to round up a social worker, but it doesn't look as though I'm going to be able to get one till Monday."

He explained that, being a weekend, Social Services were short-staffed. They had a couple of major crises to deal with, so Joe would have to wait. As if Joe didn't class as a crisis! Barrington was staring round the lounge as he spoke. Looking for something that wasn't there.

"So where is he? This boy. Joe?"

"Hiding under my bed," I said.

"Good," said Barrington, vacantly. "I'm not sure I want him to hear what I'm going to tell you. Not yet, anyway. It's all a bit strange."

A bit strange! Boy, did he have a flair for understatement! What he had to tell us was more than a bit strange; it was completely off the wall.

"The good news is," he said, "that we've traced a family of Hadleys."

"That's great," said Mum.

"What's the bad news?" asked Dad.

The detective nodded at PC Cooper to continue.

"The bad news," said Cooper, "was that it took us a while because we were looking in the wrong place. Or, rather, the right place at the wrong time. Tracing further back, we found our Hadleys exactly where our friend Joe said that we'd find them. Living here, at Moor Lane Farm, in the fifties and early sixties. They sold up late in '66."

"Wow!" shrieked Mona. "That's really weird."

"Mmm," said Barrington. "And the more you look into it, the weirder it gets. The reason they sold up was that Mr. Hadley had suffered a breakdown. Severe depression. He never got over the fact that his son had disappeared, three years earlier. They'd had a bit of an argument, apparently. Nothing serious. But the lad had gone off riding, onto the moors. The pony came back alone and the family never saw their son again."

He paused, looked at us as though we might be part of some conspiracy or hoax. As though all this was some mad scheme we'd dreamed up to waste police time!

"The boy's name was Joe," he said. "Joseph Hadley. He was eleven years old."

# Chapter Four

I went cold when they told us. It was creepy, seriously creepy. And I guess everyone else felt the same, judging by the gawping and stuttering. Everyone except Dad, that is.

And, once Dad had spelled it out for us, it sounded almost reasonable. Just because an eleven-year-old boy called Joe Hadley disappeared in 1963, it didn't mean it was our Joe, did it? It simply couldn't be, could it? According to Dad, there was nothing spooky about it. We just had to look for a logical explanation.

"If," said Dad, "a Joe Hadley really did disappear

in 1963, then I reckon our Joe must have heard the story at some time. And, for some reason, he's acting it out."

Sounded a bit unlikely to me but the cops had a similar idea.

"We've checked out people who knew the Hadleys," the detective told us. "And we're trying to trace the Hadleys themselves. The parents, who might still be alive, and the other son Peter, who was five when his brother disappeared."

Five...just like Joe had said!

"So he'll be middle-aged now," Barrington said. "Bit of a long shot but what I'm thinking is that our Joe might be related. If he was really Peter's son, he'd be familiar with the story of his Uncle Joe, wouldn't he?"

"Yeah," I said. "But why would our Joe pretend to be the old Joe?"

"Haven't a clue," said Barrington, looking a bit deflated. "Like I said, it's only an idea. The only one I can come up with at the moment."

"Unless..." I began, as another theory sprang into my mind.

Unfortunately, I didn't have time to tell anyone about it, as there was a sudden crash from upstairs. Followed by another and another.

By that time I was halfway upstairs. The noise was coming from my bedroom and no way did I want that crazy kid wrecking it, no matter who he thought he was.

As I flung open the door, a book hit me full in the face. My history book. The sort of thick, hefty thing you don't really want smacking into your nose.

The impact sent me staggering back into Mona but I soon recovered and went lurching into the room ready to throttle Joe, or whoever he was. He wasn't there but I was getting used to his tricks and dropped straight down to peer under the bed.

And there he was, of course, among the muddy football shirts, dirty socks and other yucky bits that hadn't yet found their way to the washing basket. He didn't fool me with his innocent thumb-in-mouth frightened look.

"Hey, you," I said, not exactly politely. "Come out of there."

"Don't shout at him, Bug," said Mum, who'd joined everyone else in a cluster round my bed. "You'll upset him."

"Upset him?" I said, looking at all my books and stuff scattered around the floor. "Upset him! Have you seen what he's done? He's wrecked the place."

"How can you tell?" smirked Mona. "It looks tidier than usual to me."

"Shut it!" I said, as Mum glared at me.

Then she turned to Joe and her expression changed totally. "Come on Joe," she cooed. "You can come out now. It's all right. No one's going to hurt you."

A pale streak slithered towards me. I tried to grab him but he bit me! Bit my wrist so hard that he actually drew blood! But did anyone care? No, they were all looking at Joe who was whizzing around like a rogue firework.

"Did you get frightened up here on your own?" Mum said, as Joe hurled himself into her arms. "It's all right. No harm done."

"I didn't do it," Joe whimpered. "It wasn't me. It just happened. I was under the bed and everything started shaking and things came crashing down."

"Come on," said Mum, holding Joe's hand. "Come downstairs. The policemen want to talk to you. Now, don't be scared. I won't let them hurt you."

"I'll hurt *him* if he stays around much longer," I snarled, rubbing my wrist, as we followed the procession downstairs.

Mum, of course, was in her element. Fussing round Joe. Fussing round the cops. Offering everybody tea and cake. So it was a while before we could get down to any sort of business. And, even then, it was pretty chaotic. Joe didn't like the cops very much. Wouldn't look at them. Wouldn't answer their questions directly. Would only mumble some reply if Mum repeated the question. And then the answers didn't make any sense.

Which was bad enough news in itself. The even worse news was that when the cops said Joe would have to go with them, he went absolutely wild again. Pulling away when they tried to restrain him. Curling himself up into a ball on the floor. Rocking backwards and forwards while Mum started ranting on about human rights and telling the cops to leave poor Joe alone!

What were they supposed to do? Mum gave them the answer, didn't she? She was in there volunteering, while the rest of us looked on in horror. Yes, of course Joe could stay for a couple of days until the social workers turned up. No trouble. No trouble at all. And, as Joe screamed and hurled himself about every time the cops got close to him, they eventually agreed.

Our house is pretty big. Four bedrooms. But, as one of them has been turned into an office, we don't have a spare room as such. When Mona and me have friends to stay we set up camp beds in our rooms. So guess where Joe had to sleep?

Mum said she'd clear up my bedroom if Mona

and me took the dogs out. Well, I was only too pleased to escape, but the minute we got out in the yard, we heard footsteps behind us. And there was Joe. Following us. Like another dog in the pack.

I was about to tell him to buzz off when I saw Mum standing at the door, arms folded, lips in tight no-nonsense mode, nodding at us to let Joe tag along.

And if we weren't very happy, the dogs were even worse. They're normally well behaved but that Saturday they went completely mad. All three of them alternately cowering behind our legs, almost tripping us up or running off, refusing to come back when called.

Was there anything that behaved normally around Joe, I thought, as we walked through the village with him prattling on in his stupid way.

"Where's the shop? What have they done with the village shop? I don't understand. It's my village. I know it is. But it's all wrong. What's happening? How am I going to find my mum? Where is she? How am I going to find her?"

Those are just a few of the things he said. Most of them repeated a dozen times. His voice rising to first a screech and then an absolute howl. A howl which the dogs joined in with, so our walk turned into total chaos.

"Oh, this is hopeless," moaned Mona. "Let's get him back."

Which is what we intended to do. Taking a short cut through the alleyway that brought us out in front of the cottages, on the edge of the village not far from our house. They're old farm labourers' cottages and they mainly now belong to young couples who go out to work, so you never see them much. But the last one, right on the end...well, that's the one we usually tried to hurry past.

It belongs to old Nora Tamsworth or Nutty Nora as me and Mona called her when Mum wasn't listening. I mean, Nora was okay. Harmless. And calling her names wasn't very nice, I suppose. But it's not as if we did it to her face, like some kids. In fact our trouble was that we were a bit too polite and once Nora stopped us, it was impossible to get away. She'd ramble on for hours, talking about the old days, telling you the same stories over and over.

It was Nora who had told us the legend of Demon's Rock. And it was quite interesting the first time round, I suppose. The story goes that back in the Middle Ages there were witches at work in the village. Blighting crops, causing sickness, curdling milk, the usual rubbish witches used to get blamed for.

Anyway, the locals decided to build a church with

a big spire to ward off evil...like you do. But when the Devil got to hear about it, he wasn't happy. Didn't fancy a new church on his patch. So he sent one of his fiercest demons, up from the bowels of hell, to disrupt the work.

And disrupt it he did. Stones went missing, windows got broken and the wood for the doors was set on fire. Now you and me might think that thieves and vandals were involved, but our medieval friends naturally thought that there must be a demon at work. And, with all the hysteria whipped up, it wasn't long before the villagers actually saw him sitting on top of the half-finished spire, which promptly collapsed.

The angry villagers chased the demon onto the moor where he turned on them, snarling and spitting fire. So they picked up rocks and boulders and started hurling them at the demon who crouched down, hands over his head to protect himself. But still the missiles came. So he did what any self-respecting demon might do and turned himself to stone so he couldn't be killed.

And there, according to Nutty Nora, he crouches still, surrounded by the rocks and stones that the villagers threw at him. Ready to spring into demonic action again, whenever the time is right.

Demon dealt with, the church was finished but

with a small tower instead of the huge spire... Not a bad story the first time you hear it but Nora must have told us at least a dozen times, usually finishing with:

"Only a story to be sure, but strange things happen at Demon's Rock. Always have and always will. So you keep well away. Dark forces are at work up there. Evil forces. More terrible than you could possibly imagine."

We'd nod and smile. Humour her. And she'd be off on another story. Sometimes something to do with Demon's Rock. Stuff that we used to think was completely mad.

But, more often than not, she'd tell us things about her own life and family. Typical oldie, I suppose. Remembered every detail of the school outing from eighty years back, but couldn't remember what she'd told us two minutes ago. Or even who we were. She hardly ever remembered our names. Usually called Mona "Mabel", which was the name of Nutty Nora's sister apparently. The one she used to live with. The one who died a year or so before we moved here.

Anyway, that Saturday afternoon with Joe screeching and the dogs yelping, we had no chance of sneaking past Nora's. She's supposed to be deaf so I reckon she's developed some sort of sixth sense, which tells her when someone's coming. She's wobbly on her legs too. Walks with a frame. But you'd think it was jet propelled the speed she reaches that gate sometimes.

"Mabel!" she shouted out, as we tried to rush past, tangled up in three dog leads.

"It's Mona, Miss Tamsworth," my sister pointed out.

That's how used to our nicknames we are! We even call ourselves Bug and Mona!

"Mona," said Miss Tamsworth. "Of course. And Beetle."

"Bug," I said, wondering whether she was as daft as she sometimes seemed, or whether she did that sort of thing on purpose.

Not that I had the chance to wonder for long because the next words out of her mouth stopped me dead in whatever tracks I was trying to make.

"And Joe!" Nutty Nora said, her wrinkly face cracking into a smile. "Little Joe Hadley."

Mona and I looked at each other for a moment. Had Nora somehow heard the news? That there was a kid called Joe Hadley staying with us? Had the cops been here? Had they told her? Possible. Definitely possible. They'd been making enquiries about the Hadley family, hadn't they? And who better to ask than the village's oldest resident? Even if she was several crumbs short of a biscuit.

But the funny thing was, Nora really seemed to know Joe!

"I haven't seen you for ages, Joe," she said.

"Hello, Miss Tamsworth," Joe said.

And I had to think for a second. Had we said her name? Yes. Mona had said it. So Joe was just repeating it, wasn't he? Only he smiled as he said it. Positively beamed, before his face slipped into confused mode again.

"You are Miss Tamsworth, aren't you?" he said. "I know you are. This is your house. I recognize you. Only you look...you look different. Older! Much older."

"Aye, I'm getting on a bit now," said Nutty Nora, as though this was a perfectly ordinary conversation. "I'll be ninety-three next birthday. They keep telling me I'll have to move out soon. Into one of those homes. But I'm not going."

"Ninety-three," Joe repeated, ignoring the rest.

He stared at me, then at Mona, then back to Nutty Nora and all the time his eyes were sort of flickering as if he were trying to work something out.

"But," said Joe, "you can't be. You can't have got that old. Not so quickly. Not like this. I saw you last

Sunday. In church. You were there."

"Was I?" said Nora. "Last Sunday? It seems longer than that to me. But maybe you're right. I get confused these days. I don't always remember."

"You were all right then," Joe gabbled. "You didn't look like this! You didn't have a walking frame. You didn't have white hair."

"I used to have auburn hair," said Nora, with the funny smile she always has when she drifts off to the past. "Beautiful auburn hair."

"I know," said Joe. "I know! Tied up in a bun at the back. Going a bit grey at the front but it was still nice," he added.

"Thank you, dear," said Nora. "You were always such a polite boy. And you haven't changed a bit, Joe. Not one little bit."

As I said, poor Nora had lost more than a few marbles over the years. Nuttier than a bag of peanuts. So maybe she didn't find it at all strange that Joe was still eleven while she'd aged by forty years or so!

Well obviously not, judging by her next question.

"And how's that little scamp of a brother of yours?" she said. "How's young Peter?"

"I don't know," said Joe, with the panicky edge to his voice, setting the dogs off pawing and pulling again. "I don't know. I can't find him. He's not here."

"Oh, he's a terror for running off, isn't he?" said Nora. "Well, you'd better go and find him or your dad'll be after you!"

"But I can't find Dad either," Joe wailed. "Or Mum."

"Oh," said Nora. "Well that's it, then, isn't it? They've probably all popped out to the shops. I'm sure they'll be back soon."

"You don't understand," said Joe. "They've gone. Completely gone. These people are there instead. Living in my house."

He pointed accusingly at us.

"Oh no," said Nora. "That can't be right. Mabel lives here with me. But I don't know who the other one is."

Mona shook her head as she always did when Nora confused her with Mabel. I mean, we'd seen the photos and Mona doesn't look anything like the young Mabel. But who could tell what went on in Nora's befuddled brain sometimes?

"Look," I said, seeing Joe getting more and more agitated, "I'm sorry, Miss Tamsworth. We have to go now."

We set off, the dogs pulling in front, Joe trailing behind, looking back at Nora. Then trotting to catch up with us. Sort of excited and miserable all at the same time.

"She knows me," he muttered. "She's the same but different. And she knows me."

"She's bonkers," said Mona. "Doesn't know who she's talking to half the time. Thinks I'm her flaming sister, for heaven's sake! So you must have reminded her of someone."

"But," Joe insisted, "she knows Peter. She knows Mum and Dad. She recognizes me. And...I don't understand..."

He paused, turned, then stood looking back, muttering to himself. I walked on, leaving Mona to deal with Joe.

Okay, I decided, so the fact that Nora knew the old Hadleys would make sense. But why, among her many tales, hadn't she ever told us about them?

The fact that she'd accepted Joe wasn't, I decided, as bizarre as it first seemed. Past and present often merge into one in Nora's mind. And if the cops were right, if Joe was Peter's son, there'd be a family resemblance, wouldn't there? Even more of one, if my own idea was right.

"I've had a thought," I whispered to Mona. "About Joe."

Unfortunately Joe heard me say his name, so I had to shut up.

Dad didn't want to say too much in front of Joe

either. When we got back he told us that the cops had phoned but waited until after dinner to tell us exactly what they'd had to say. Shoving us into the lounge, leaving Joe safely in the kitchen with Mum, or so we thought.

"The police have traced the Hadleys," Dad said. "They live in Cumbria now but Joe isn't a relative. Or, at least, not one they're admitting to. Peter Hadley's married with three grown-up daughters but no sons."

"Yeah, but I've been thinking about that," I said.

"Just let me finish," said Dad. "Old Mrs. Hadley lives with Peter and his family but Mr. Hadley's in a nursing home. Remember the police said he'd suffered a breakdown when Joe went missing? Well, the poor man never really recovered. Started drinking heavily. Had one breakdown after another, apparently. Each one worse than the last. Got so bad that his wife couldn't cope with him at home. He even tried to kill himself a couple of times and now...well now, he doesn't speak, barely eats...he's just quietly wasting away."

"*No!*" came the shout from the doorway, two seconds before Joe burst in, hurling himself at Dad, lashing out with his feet. "It isn't true. It isn't true!"

How long had he been standing there? How much had he heard? Quite a lot by the sound of his ravings.

"That's not my dad you're talking about. My dad never drank! It isn't my Peter. It can't be. He's not grown up. He's not married. You've done something to them, haven't you? You've hidden them. You've murdered them!"

Oh great, I thought, as Joe hurled himself onto the floor and started rolling round in complete hysteria. So we're murderers now, are we? Fantastic.

"So what was your idea, Bug?" Mona asked, dragging me to one side as Mum rushed in and kneeled beside the writhing Joe.

"Oh, that," I said. "Well, we know Joe isn't Peter Hadley's son, right?"

Mona nodded.

"So what if he's *Joe* Hadley's son?"

"Hang about," said Mona. "You mean the Joe Hadley who disappeared?"

"Yeah," I said. "I mean, they never found a body or anything, did they? There's nothing to say that he died back in 1963, is there? What if he ran away? Or was abducted by someone? Grew up. Had a kid."

"It's possible," said Mona, slowly. "But it still doesn't explain why this Joe's turned up here, does it? Or why he's pretending to be the original Joe."

Well, no it didn't. But, in a way, I was starting to get quite caught up in it all. Even thinking it might be interesting to have Joe around for a while. Mystery to solve and all that. Bug and Mona...private detectives! Amazing the police with their powers of deduction.

Only my enthusiasm didn't last long because that night something happened. Something that changed my mind about everything, entirely.

# Chapter Five

"**I** thought Joe could have your bed, Bug," Mum informed me. "Poor thing didn't get any sleep last night. You can have the camp bed."

Wonderful! Especially as it didn't look as though Joe was going to get any sleep that night either, whatever bed he was in. He was still restless. Muttering about Nora, the village and his parents. Examining the duvet. Asking if he could have some proper blankets. Pulling the duvet cover off, diving inside, using it like a sleeping bag. Changing his mind. Shuffling about. Muttering again.

"It isn't true. None of it's true. It isn't happening. It can't be. It *can't* be."

"Go to sleep, then," I snapped. "And when you wake up it'll all be back to normal."

Well, I'd have said anything to shut him up! And it seemed as though he believed me. Or wanted to believe me, at any rate, because within seconds he'd settled down. Snuffling and whimpering in his sleep.

I guess I must have drifted off too because I don't remember anything else until the camp bed collapsed.

It does it all the time. Buckles in the middle of the night like that. We'd kept meaning to get it fixed but had never got round to it. So, for a moment, I didn't think anything of it. Just groaned, rolled over and resigned myself to sleeping a little closer to the floor.

Except that the floor was shaking. Trembling like the plates on the dresser had done. Only it didn't feel like a minor quake this time. It felt mega. Like those earthquakes you see on the news, where whole buildings collapse!

It felt hot too. The whole room was stuffy, stifling, choking.

How long did it take for all the information to filter through? I don't know. Fractions of a second maybe. And in that instant, as my eyes opened wide, I saw the bed. My bed. It was on fire.

What had he done? Where was he? Still in the bed? I didn't know. I couldn't see. All the possibilities, all the things you're supposed to do in the case of fire flashed through my mind, but my body reacted all on its own. My mouth screaming in terror, my arms picking up my duvet, hurling it onto the bed, trying to fight down the flames.

"Call 999!" I yelled as footsteps raced towards my room and the door was flung open. "He's started a fire! He's started a fire!"

And all the time I was beating down with the duvet, ignoring all the screams and shouts that mingled with my own, until hands gripped my shoulders, dragging me away.

"Bug!" my mother screamed, whirling me round to face her. "Bug, stop it! What are you trying to do?"

"He tried to kill me," I heard Joe yell. "He threw that thing over me. Tried to smother me."

"What do you expect if you start a fi—"

I stopped, literally mid-word. Knowing something was wrong. Very wrong. I pulled myself away from Mum. Swung round towards the bed. And there was Joe, thumb in mouth, eyes screwed tight shut, hunched up against the pillows, duvet pulled up to his chin. Not a mark on any of them. No heat. No flames. No trembling floor. No fire.

"It was on fire," I began. "The bed was on fire!"

"You had a dream, Bug," said Dad, looking at the collapsed camp bed.

"It wasn't a dream," I said, staring at Joe.

"Of course it was," said Mum. "What else could it have been?"

"Him," I muttered. "Something to do with him."

"Don't be ridiculous, Bug," Mum snapped, as she fixed the camp bed. "Now go on. Get back to sleep. The pair of you."

Mona, who'd been standing by the door, still half asleep, shrugged and wandered off. Mum and Dad waited until I'd got back into bed then followed Mona, switching off the light.

And I might have done what Mum said. I might have dismissed it all as a dream. Gone straight back to sleep. But something made me look up. Towards the bed. And there was Joe. Still sitting propped up against the pillow. His body shimmering pink and orange. His eyes wide open. Shining in the dark. Red eyes. Mad eyes. Unnatural eyes.

I shrieked, rolled out of bed and hurled myself at the door just as it opened. So I fell into Dad's arms.

"What is it now?" Mum asked as she hovered impatiently behind us. "I didn't even have time to get back to bed."

"Never mind that!" I yelled. "Look at him! *Look* at him!"

By that time Mum had switched on the bedroom light and was looking at Joe, as instructed.

A Joe with ordinary blue eyes. A perfectly normal Joe.

Only, just as the shrieks died on my lips, Joe kicked off, didn't he? Screams of terror that brought Mona rushing back as well.

"No!" Joe yelled. "It's not fair! You're still here! What's happening? It was all back. My room. My house. I saw my mum. I saw her. She was here. This was my room again. And now it's not. Who are you? Why are you doing this?"

"Never mind what *we're* doing," I yelled back. "What are *you* doing? Who are you?"

"Oh, for goodness' sake, Bug," said Mum. "Calm down. You've been dreaming. Both of you."

"I don't want him here," I said. "I'm not going back to sleep with him in here."

"Right," said Dad, folding up the camp bed. "You can sleep in our room. Just for tonight. Just so we can all get some peace."

Peace! Little did he know. Little did any of us know.

\*

I opted to have the camp bed plonked in Mona's room, while Mum and Dad went back to settle Joe.

"It happened," I whispered to Mona. "It really happened. I didn't dream it. His eyes were red. Completely red. Burning."

"Shut it, Bug," her voice snapped back through the darkness. "Or I'll be having nightmares too."

"It wasn't a nightmare! I don't know who he is or what he's doing here but I don't think...I don't think...he's human."

"Don't be stupid," she hissed. "You're giving me the creeps! Of course he's human. What else could he be?"

A question that kept me awake for most of the night. I didn't reach any conclusions, of course, but wherever my mind took me, I kept coming back to the same point. That what I'd seen in my room was similar to what Joe had described up on the moor. That it was all, somehow, connected to Demon's Rock.

Crazy as it seemed, the disappearing Joe, our Joe, the tremors, the vibrations that sent plates crashing, the flames that didn't burn, the red eyes, the moors, the rock...were all tied up together. But how?

Nothing made sense. There wasn't a single sane fact that I could hook on to. Nothing in the realms of normal experience that could explain any of it. So I started straying into the abnormal, didn't I?

I won't even tell you some of the stupid ideas that went through my head. Just the one. The one that seemed quite reasonable in the middle of the night. The one I woke Mona up to tell her about.

"How about this?" I said. "Joe Hadley rides off onto the moors in 1963, right?"

"Right," Mona groaned.

"So, what if he was abducted...by aliens?"

"Aliens!" Mona hissed. "Get real."

"You read about things like that," I insisted. "They might have taken him away, but kept him frozen or something. Exactly as he was. Experimented on him. Given him superhuman powers. Then sent him back..."

· "Don't be pathetic!"

"Or maybe," I persisted, "Joe grew up. Interbred with his alien captors. Produced our Joe. That would make more sense."

"Interesting idea of sense you've got," Mona yawned.

"And the burning rock he thought he saw could have been a spaceship."

"Bug!" said Mona. "*Shut up!*"

I couldn't really blame Mona. My ideas sounded

a bit mad, eh? But crazy things do happen sometimes. They *were* happening. To us. But why? The question was in my mind as I finally drifted off to sleep and it was still there in the morning when I woke.

Mona's bed was empty. I had no idea what time it was because the clocks still weren't working and it was cloudy outside, so it was hard to tell. But I guessed it was pretty late. I headed back to my room to get my clothes, pausing outside the door. Reluctant to go in. Scared of what I might see. Was he in there? Or had he already gone downstairs?

I was still standing there, wondering, when Mona came upstairs, clutching Joe's clothes.

"Give him these," she said, throwing them to me. "They're dry now."

I caught the clothes but, as I did, some sweets and a few coins rolled onto the floor. Out of the trouser pocket, I guess.

"Weird," said Mona, picking up the coins. "What's he doing with foreign money?"

Only the coins weren't foreign, were they?

"No, wait a minute," said Mona. "Look at this, Bug."

She handed me a little silver coin about the size of a five-pence piece. It had the Queen's head. A very young-looking queen. And a date. 1955.

"It's a sixpence," I said.

Not a brilliant piece of deduction as it had the name written on the coin and, besides, I'd seen one before. But it still made me shudder.

"It's old money," I said. "My history teacher brought some in once."

"Wow," said Mona. "Look at this penny. It's huge! And dead old. It hasn't even got the Queen on, look. It's a king. George VI. And a halfpenny. Fancy having halfpennies! I wonder what those are worth in our money? I'm going to show Dad. He'll know."

"Mona!" I said. "Never mind what they're worth. Think about it. I mean, don't you think it's a touch odd, that Joe's walking about with a pocketful of old coins? After what he told us, after..."

"Hey," said Mona, laughing, "you don't really believe all that rubbish you were droning on about last night, do you? About Joe being abducted by aliens back in 1963?"

"I don't know," I said. "I don't know what I believe any more. After what I saw. But he's not...he's not normal, Mona. That's for sure."

Mona looked at me. Trying to work out whether I was winding her up.

"I mean it," I said. "Look, don't show Dad. Just put the coins back, eh?"

"Why?"

"I'm not sure," I said. "I just don't think we should mess with any of Joe's things. Not until we find out exactly what's going on."

"Maybe we won't ever find out," said Mona. "I mean, he'll probably be going tomorrow, won't he? With the social workers. Then we won't have to worry about him, will we? We can just forget all about him."

If only! If only any of that had turned out to be true.

# Chapter Six

It wasn't even possible to forget about Joe for two minutes because, when I finally plucked up the courage to push open the bedroom door, my bedroom wasn't there! Well, it was. In a way. But it was shimmering. Moving. Flickering. Like a giant hologram. Shifting out of focus. Fading.

"Mona!" I shouted, never taking my eyes off the room.

Watching it settle back to normality in the minute or so it took Mona to sprint back upstairs.

"What?" she said, pausing in the doorway as a lumpy shape thrashed around under the duvet, emerging dazed and sleepy.

I hurled the clothes at Joe and slammed the door, holding it shut.

"Don't go in there," I told Mona. "Don't go in there at all. Not while he's here."

"Bug," she said, as Joe hammered on the door. "Have you gone mad, or what? Let him out."

I moved away from the door, dragging Mona back with me towards the stairs. And out Joe came. Looking fairly normal except that he was shaking his head violently from side to side.

"This is the dream," he said, putting his hands up and gripping himself by the throat, digging his grubby nails into his neck. "This is still the dream."

"I'll get Mum," said Mona, bolting downstairs.

"Okay," I hissed at him. "You can quit the act now. What do you think you're doing? Who are you?"

"I'm Joe," he said, bursting into tears, dropping to his knees and bashing his head on the floor.

Deliberately. Over and over. Bashing his head. Screaming his name.

"I'm Joe. I'm Joe. Leave me alone!"

It was all my fault, of course. According to Mum. I'd upset him, hadn't I? So I didn't even tell her about the room. What was the point? There wasn't a chance of her believing me, was there?

I told Mona though, who looked as though she didn't know whether to laugh or get me to the nearest psychiatrist.

"So what are you saying now?" she asked in the end. "That he's some sort of illusionist? Or is he using his alien powers perhaps?"

"I don't know," I said, as Mona shook her head. "I don't know. But whoever he is, I intend to find out."

Just how I was going to do that, I wasn't sure. But after lunch, when Mum was looking for a volunteer to take Nutty Nora her Sunday afternoon treat, I decided that was probably a good place to start.

"I'll come with you," said Mona.

Mum looked at us, suspiciously. Every week she'd buy a Sunday paper and a bit of chocolate or something for Nora. Every week she'd try to persuade one of us to take them round and usually end up taking them herself. Now she had both of us volunteering.

"What are you up to, Bug?" Mona asked, as we headed down the lane. "Why are you suddenly so keen to see Nora?"

"I'm not up to anything," I said. "I just thought I might be able to get her talking about the Hadleys, that's all."

"There's no point," said Mona. "You know what she's like!"

Well, sure. There wasn't *much* chance of getting any sense out of her. It would all depend on what sort of mood she was in. What century she'd chosen to live in that day. But, in the absence of any better ideas, it seemed worth a try.

It started well enough. She recognized us! Actually greeted us as Bug and Mona. Invited us in. Offered us some lemonade. Okay, so what she actually gave us was cups of none-too-warm tea, but that was fairly good by Nora's standards. Unfortunately, no sooner were the cups in our hands than Nora took the photo of her parents off the mantelpiece.

"Do you remember seeing us yesterday?" I asked, trying to head her off before she could get started on one of her family stories.

"Yesterday?" she said, screwing up her wrinkled forehead. "Yesterday? Yes, I think so."

"With Joe," I said. "Joe Hadley."

She gasped so heavily and sank into her chair so quickly that I thought, for one horrible moment, she was having a fit or a heart attack.

"Joe Hadley," she breathed. "How do you know about Joe?"

So, she hadn't remembered. Bit disappointing, but there was still a chance we might get something out of her.

"We heard the story," I said. "About how he disappeared."

"Don't!" said Nora, clutching the side of the chair. "Don't say it. Don't tell me. I don't want to hear about it again. It was my fault. It was all my fault."

Her fault? Nora's fault? What was going on? Was she about to confess to a murder or kidnap or something? The business with our Joe had got me so jumpy, I was more or less prepared to believe anything.

"I'm sure it wasn't, Miss Tamsworth," said Mona, who still had some sort of grip on reality. "It can't have been."

"He was always doing it," said Nora, staring at us. "Always riding off onto those moors on his own. I tried to tell him. I tried to warn him. I told his parents. But they just laughed. They all laughed. They didn't understand. I should have made them see. It was my fault. I should have made them understand."

"Understand what?" I asked.

"The evil," she said.

Even from across the room, I could see her start to tremble.

"The evil at Demon's Rock," she said.

Well, we'd heard it all before, of course. How there were supposed to be dark forces at work up there. And we'd always shrugged it off as the ravings of a nutter. But now...well, now things were different.

"What sort of evil?" I asked.

"People don't believe any more," she said, by way of an answer. "They don't believe in heaven and hell. They don't believe in the dark one. In hell fire. But I've seen it. I've seen him at work! Up there by his rock. It was a long time ago. I was only sixteen. But I remember."

Well, obviously I didn't believe in demons and all that rot, but there was something familiar about what she was saying. The mention of the rock and fire. A closeness to Joe's story that made me want to know more.

"What do you remember?" I asked. "What happened?"

She shook her head, fingering the cross and chain she always wore around her neck, then looked down at the photo of her parents that was resting on her knees.

"Mother warned me," Nora said. "She warned me about boys. Said they were only after one thing."

Mona pulled a face. Convinced, like I was, that

we'd lost her. That Nora was off on a tangent. Some boring family story.

"But I thought George was different," she said. "So I sneaked out one Sunday afternoon."

Mona and I grinned at each other. It was almost impossible to imagine Miss Tamsworth as a teenager at all. Let alone a rebellious one!

"We went walking," she was saying. "Up on the moor. But when it started getting dark, he wouldn't turn back. He wouldn't take me home. He tried to...he tried to..."

The story was getting a bit yucky and I wasn't at all sure I wanted to hear all the gory details of what George tried to do, but once Nora gets started she doesn't stop.

"He tried to...kiss me!" Nora said.

I almost breathed a sigh of relief. Was that it? A kiss! Pretty daring for the 1930s or whenever it was, maybe, but hardly headline scandal!

"I thumped him," said Nora, as Mona laughed. "And he ran off. I had to find my own way back. In the dark. With a storm brewing up. I stumbled. Fell over. And that's when it happened. That's when I saw it!"

We were back to the original story so quickly, I almost missed it.

"Saw what?" I squeaked.

"The flames," she said. "The terrible flames."

Miss Tamsworth clutched the photo in her bent hands, as Mona and I waited for her to go on.

"Mother was angry when I got home all frightened and dirty," Nora said. "She said what I'd seen were his flames. Hell, opening up, ready to swallow me for being so wicked."

Wicked? No wonder poor Nora had never married. If she'd been told that the jaws of hell would open up at the first hint of a kiss!

But, if not the jaws of hell, what *had* she seen up there? What had Joe seen?

"I was lucky," said Nora, staring intently at us. "I got away. But you'd be surprised how many people have gone missing up there over the years."

Well, no, I wouldn't. Those moors are treacherous. It's easy to get lost. It only takes a mist coming down or a snowstorm. And by "years" Nora meant centuries. She'd told us tales before of people going missing. Making out that they were big mysteries though most had pretty obvious explanations. The young girl in the eighteenth century who disappeared on the way to her wedding.

Nothing to do with the fact that it was an arranged marriage to a grumpy old miser in his sixties, of course! I mean, who could blame her for running away? Then there was the soldier from the nineteenth century who disappeared leaving massive debts behind him. Well, not hard to work that one out!

But putting it all together with what Nora claimed to have seen, with what Joe had described, with what I'd seen myself, with my own eyes...there was a connection. There had to be. As I told Mona on the way home.

"Since when," said Mona, "have you believed anything Nora says? And Joe...well, he's obviously had some sort of accident, hasn't he? Concussion. Shock or something."

"What about me?" I insisted. "What about what I saw?"

Mona opened her mouth to speak and I could tell, by the look on her face, that she was about to dismiss it all as dream, hallucination, madness.

"Plates and books flying around?" I pressed on. "The way the dogs react, the clocks, the coins in Joe's pocket? Is that all in my mind too?"

"No, but it's coincidence, isn't it? Okay, then," she said, as I shook my head. "Go on. What do you reckon?"

"I don't know!" I shouted. "But I meant what I said about Joe last night."

"About him being genetically modified by

aliens?" Mona sneered. "Or the result of a very mixed marriage!"

"Maybe not that, exactly but..."

I never got to finish. We'd reached home by that point. And, even before we opened the gate, we could hear the shrieks. Following the sound, looking up to the window of the spare room, we saw the outline of two figures. The small one hurling himself at the larger one. It was Joe and he was attacking my dad!

By the time we'd raced up there, Dad was slumped on the chair in front of the computer and Mum had got Joe under some sort of control.

"It's all right," Dad said, as we burst in. "It's all right now."

"What happened?" I said, staring at the scratch mark on Dad's cheek.

A long, deep scratch.

"What did he do?" Mona asked.

"He came in when I was doing my e-mails," said Dad, sort of half smiling. "Got a bit excited by the computer. Seemed really frightened by it. Started yelping and pulling all the leads out. Flipped when I tried to stop him."

"It's only a computer, Joe," Mum was saying. "You must have computers at school, love."

"The school's not there!" Joe yelled. "It's gone. Everything's gone."

"Like his brain," I muttered.

"And all these new things," he screamed. "That funny telly you write on! The typewriter that doesn't have a ribbon! I don't like it! I don't like it! It's all wrong."

"Not much of an advanced alien, is he?" Mona hissed. "If he doesn't even know what a keyboard is."

"Alien?" Mum hissed back. "Don't be ridiculous! Honestly, I don't know what's got into you two!"

"Us?" I said, as I watched a trail of blood trickle down Dad's cheek. "It's not us who's wrecking stuff and attacking people, is it?"

And then, just as Mum launched into a defence of Joe, a horrible thought struck me. What if the Demon's Rock business was leading us down a false trail? What if all that was the same legendary rubbish it had always been?

What if the real answer was a lot simpler? What if Joe was ill? What if he had some terrible disease that affected the brain? CJD or rabies or some weird, unknown virus? A contagious disease! One that could be transmitted by contact.

He'd bitten me, hadn't he? Drawn blood. And it was after that I'd started to see things like the fire and my room shifting about. Started to have all my crazy ideas about Demon's Rock and aliens. What if he'd infected me? What if I was going mad?

"Er, Dad," I said, as soon as Mum had finished. "I think you ought to see a doctor about that scratch. And my wrist's still a bit sore."

"Put some cream on," he said, rubbing his cheek. "That's what I'm going to do. It'll soon heal up."

He was right, too. His scratch did disappear. So did my bite mark. Much quicker than we'd expected. Which was bad news. Really bad news. Because, after what happened, those injuries were just the sort of evidence I needed.

# Chapter Seven

My injury was still bothering me when I went to bed, though.

"I don't mind you camping out on my floor again," said Mona. "But will you stop playing with that torch and go to sleep?"

"I'm not playing," I told her. "I'm looking at my bite. It's getting worse. It's definitely getting worse. It's all swollen and red, look."

"I've seen it," she yawned. "About fifty times in the last two hours. You've done nothing but fret about it all night!"

Well, it was all right for her, wasn't it? She wasn't

the one who was infected. And nobody but me was taking it seriously. My parents had accused me of attention seeking! And Dad had laughed when I'd insisted on watching the news to see if there was a new virus going round. Or whether dozens of Joes had been set loose on the world as part of some bizarre biological attack. Needless to say, they hadn't.

Even so, I got Mum to check my temperature. It was normal, she said. But it didn't feel normal and it didn't stop me worrying. Watching the redness slowly spreading.

"Why don't you check your palms while you're at it?" Mona said. "See if you've grown any hair. You never know, he might be a werewolf...oh, for heaven's sake, Bug! I didn't mean it," she squealed.

It's supposed to be a sign of madness, isn't it? Looking for hairs on the palms of your hands. The next sign is finding some but, mercifully, I didn't.

"Of course there's nothing there, you eejit," Mona said when I told her. "Now shut up and go to sleep."

She didn't really need to tell me. My eyes were so heavy I could barely keep them open, even though my brain was still buzzing with questions and possibilities. The stuff nightmares are made of.

Which is why, when I first heard the screaming, I

thought it was exactly that. A nightmare. It was too intense, too terrible to be real. But Mona had heard it too. The screams, the banging, coming from the room next door. My bedroom.

We both leaped up, darted out and saw Mum and Dad heading towards the bedroom door. My first instinct was to stop them. Throwing myself at the door, standing in front of it, clutching the handle, barring their way.

"Don't go in there," I yelled. "It's not safe."

"Don't be ridiculous, Bug," Mum snapped. "Of course it's safe. Let me in. Joe's having another nightmare, that's all."

But the image of my bedroom, distorting like it had done that morning, was so strong that I refused to budge. Shouting at them to stand back, as I felt the doorknob burning in my hand.

It was the heat, rather than my parents' pleas, which made me pull away. As soon as I moved, my parents were there, pushing open the door, gasping at what they saw.

The room was wrecked again. But rather than the heat I'd expected, it was freezing. The window open, curtains blowing with rain darting in, splashing onto the bed. The empty bed. There was no sign of Joe. Not even when we checked in the wardrobe and under the bed.

"What's he been doing? What's going on?" said Dad, as he picked up a few items from the floor.

"And where's he gone?" said Mona, shivering by the window. "Do you reckon he could have slithered down the drainpipe? It's come away from the wall a bit, look."

"But why?" said Mum. "Why would he leave like this? In the middle of the night? Through the window. He must have been terrified. Something must have scared him. But what?"

Who could say? Nothing Joe did, nothing about him, made any sense.

"We'll have to find him," said Mum. "Bug, Mona, get dressed. Just throw some clothes on over your night things."

"No way," I said. "No way am I going out."

"Why do we need to go at all?" said Mona. "Just call the police."

"I will," said Mum. "If we don't find him right away. But he can't have been gone long. We're sure to catch up, if we get a move on."

After a search of the garden and sheds revealed nothing, we split up. Took two cars. Mum and Mona heading off through the village. Me and Dad driving towards the moor. As Mum suspected, Joe hadn't got far. In fact, as soon as we rounded the first bend up the steep hill, we spotted him. All soggy and frozen in the glare of our headlamps.

I tried to phone Mum but couldn't get a signal and by the time I got out of the car to give Dad a hand, Joe was in full rant mode.

"Leave me alone!" he was shouting, as Dad tried to guide him the few steps to the car. "I have to go. I have to go back."

He pulled, squirmed, wriggled and kicked, shouting all the time above the sound of the wind.

"I have to go back to Demon's Rock. I know what's happened. I understand now."

Well, terrific. I was glad somebody did! Not that Joe was actually going to share his information with us. And I doubt whether we'd have got him into the car at all if Mum and Mona hadn't turned up. It was strange how he always settled down for Mum. Sort of deliberate. Like he wanted to keep her on side.

It worked, of course. By the time we got home we were all cold, miserable, soaked and totally exhausted but it was Joe who got the attention. It was like Mum was under some sort of spell! As though she couldn't see us at all. Only Joe.

Mum dried him off, wrapped him in a spare duvet and put him on the settee with a hot-water bottle and a drink, intending to sit with him through the night. Dad eventually went back to bed while me and Mona sat up in her room for ages, whispering in the dark.

"He'll be gone tomorrow, thank goodness," was the last thing I heard Mona say before I finally drifted off to sleep.

Being half-term we might have got a decent lie-in, except that the phone woke us. Dad had already left for work but we could hear Mum's voice in the hall, chattering into the phone and the word "Joe" cropping up every few seconds.

"Social workers," she informed us when we crawled down in search of breakfast. "They'll be here by midday."

Even Mum looked a bit relieved and I positively felt like cheering until the phone rang again.

"Hi, Jenny," Mum said.

Warning signals. Jenny's the receptionist at the vet's surgery where Mum works.

"Well, I don't know," Mum said. "It's a bit awkward."

It was obvious what was going on. Not least because it happens every single holiday. Mum books a week off. Someone phones to say there's a crisis at work and off she goes. Mona and I just can't compete with a sick sheep.

"Perhaps just for an hour," she said ignoring my frantic leaping and head-shaking. "If it's that desperate."

"Well, I hope you're taking Joe with you," I snapped as she put the phone down.

She peered round the door to the lounge where Joe was still dead to the world on the settee.

"It's a shame to wake him," she said. "I gave him some medicine earlier, so I'm sure he'll sleep through."

"And if he doesn't? If he wakes up and kicks off again? You know what he's like! He's a complete nutter!"

"I won't be long, honest. And if he wakes, you can phone me. Now don't start, Bug," she said, seeing the look on my face.

"But he's dangerous," I wailed.

"Stop being silly, Bug," she said briskly. "He's *not* dangerous."

"Oh, no," I said. "Look at my wrist! Look what he did to that. It's come up in a big lump now."

"Bug, will you stop fussing about a tiny little mark! I've had enough of this. Just leave Joe alone. He's not dangerous. He's a confused and frightened little boy who happens to be fast asleep. So all you have to do is keep an eye on him and phone me the minute he stirs. Surely you can manage that?"

It sounded easy enough but was actually quite tricky. Keeping an eye on him was okay but dead boring because we didn't dare do anything in case we woke him up. So we sat there, in silence, staring at a blank TV screen, not even daring to read a book in case the flap of pages woke him.

Every so often I looked at my watch. Pointless as it wasn't working. So I had no idea of how much time was passing. An hour? Two hours?

All that time Joe lay totally still, but suddenly he moved. Rolling over in his sleep, arms thrashing about. Should we phone Mum? But already it was too late.

The settee shook violently. Joe was thrown onto the floor, though, amazingly, he didn't wake. Amazing because it wasn't just the settee that was shaking now, it was the whole room. A vase of flowers crashed to the floor as a table toppled over. Piano keys smashed down all on their own, filling the room with their noise, drowning out our squeals. Ornaments and books bounced down from shelves. And all in an instant. Before we could even begin to react.

When we did, it was almost impossible to stand, let alone walk. It was like being on one of those crazy fairground things where the floor wobbles and shakes.

It might be fun at a fair but it's not fun in your own house especially when wide, gaping cracks start opening up in the walls.

Even worse, in a way, was the shimmering. The whole room was flickering in and out of focus, a mass of wavy light that made me feel sick and sent me crashing to my knees.

Mona did better than me. Crawling over to where the telephone lay on the floor. Grabbing the receiver. Bashing the button over and over.

"No tone," she shrieked. "Where's your mobile?"

Mobile. Pocket. Why hadn't I thought of that?

Not that it helped. It was dead. Totally dead. And all the time I was stabbing at lifeless buttons, the room was rolling around, sliding me across the floor past the still sleeping Joe, towards the door.

As I reached it, the door swung open cracking against my head. But, somehow, I managed to catch hold of it, pull myself up, and throw myself forward into the hall. It didn't help. It wasn't just the lounge that was moving, it was the whole house. The whole street, the whole country, the whole world could be on the move for all I knew.

Mona was shouting, calling out for me but I didn't go back. Help, normality, if any was to be found, would come from outside, I was sure. Maybe out there my mobile would work. Maybe out there I could alert a neighbour. If only I could turn the lock, exert enough force to open the front door before I fell over again. But the door seemed to be fighting against me. Resisting me, draining my strength.

With one final effort, I gripped the handle, pulled and stared, for a moment, in sheer terror. Because what was outside was far worse than anything that was inside. So bad that I immediately slammed the door shut, locked it, collapsed against it, barely breathing. The shock, of what I'd seen, or rather what I hadn't seen, stamping itself on my brain in great, heavy, rhythmic thuds.

Blackness. *Thud*. Emptiness. *Thud*. Nothingness. *Thud*. Void. *Thud*. My brain seeing what my eyes no longer saw. Some sort of huge black hole stretching to eternity and beyond.

The world had disappeared. There was nothing out there. Nothing left. We were totally alone.

# Chapter Eight

My brain, my body, might have collapsed, shut down completely with the sheer shock if it hadn't been for the shout. Mona calling my name over and over. Forcing me to lurch forward and hurl myself back into the lounge.

"It's him!" Mona screamed. "I'm sure he's doing all this. Somehow. In his sleep. But I can't wake him. He won't wake up!"

I'm not proud of what I did next. I've never hurt anybody before. Never. But I was terrified. Desperate. So I started kicking him. With Mona screeching at me all the time to stop. On the third or fourth kick, he woke. Rolled away from the kicks, then crouched, like an animal, his face contorted, his eyes burning red, his whole body surrounded by that shimmering light again.

"Get away from me," he growled.

Mona clutched me, trying to pull me back. But, at that moment, the room lurched again and we were both thrown forward onto Joe, forming a pile of tangled, thrashing limbs.

"I'm going to kill you!" said Joe in that same low growl that didn't sound like him at all. "I'm going to kill you."

Luckily we were both bigger than Joe and, somehow, managed to pin him down, Mona lying on his legs, me controlling his arms. But only for a moment. As the movement of the room settled, Joe sprang up with an impossible burst of energy, knocking us over, chanting his threat again.

"I'm going to kill you. I'm going to kill you."

Some reflex action had made me hold onto his arm. I was still holding it when Joe bounded to the far side of the room. An arm. Just an arm. Ripped from his shoulder. I threw it down, watching it burn up on the carpet while the whole room echoed with screams. My screams, Mona's screams, Joe's screams.

How long did it go on? I'm not sure. Mona must

have broken free of the hysteria first because the next thing I knew she was kneeling beside me, slapping my face. Telling me to listen. To look.

But what was I listening to? There was no noise. Then I realized. That was it. The silence. The stillness.

The vibrations, the noise, the movement had stopped. And there was Joe, cowering against the far wall. All his limbs in place. Both arms slack by his side. His eyes pale and exhausted.

Mona pulled me up and we all stood, for a moment, looking at the room and at each other. Joe seeming as confused as we were. All of us trying to grasp what was real, what was illusion.

The state of the room told me that the tremors, at least, had been real. But the detached, burning arm? Illusion, obviously. And the void? The blackness outside? The light in the room told me illusion. But I raced to the window just to be sure. Stared out at the familiar scene. Flopped down on the window seat as my legs gave way. Mona backed away from Joe, never taking her eyes off him, coming to sit beside me.

"Who is he?" she breathed. "What's happening?"

An image popped into my mind.

"That guy," I said. "On TV. That mind-control bloke. Illusionist. He can do weird stuff like that. Maybe Joe..."

"No," said Joe. "It's not me. I'm not doing it."

Mona grabbed my mobile from my pocket as Joe moved towards us.

"Wait," he said, stopping again. "It's not me but I think I know. I think I can explain."

Mona ignored him, frantically bashing buttons, throwing the phone down in frustration as it refused to respond.

"I saw it," said Joe. "Yesterday. Last night. Like a dream. But it wasn't a dream."

"Don't come any closer," I said.

He didn't look wild or dangerous any more but I wasn't taking any chances.

"I knew," said Joe. "I knew before. But I couldn't make myself believe it. It wasn't possible. But I'm sure now."

"Sure of what?" said Mona.

"This isn't my time," said Joe.

"Yeah, right," I said. "You were born in 1952!"

"I was," he said. "But there was an accident. At Demon's Rock. I'm supposed to be here but not *now*. It's the right place but the wrong time. They're trying to send me back. But it won't work. Not here. I have to go back to the rock. It'll work there. They can put it right."

"They?" said Mona.

"I saw them," said Joe. "Last night. They were trying then. But it didn't work! It didn't work. You brought me back. You wouldn't let me go."

He'd been moving towards the door as he spoke, so I jumped up, raced over, stood in front of it.

"And we're still not letting you go," I said. "You're staying right here till Mum gets back."

"You don't understand," he said. "It's going to get worse. Me being here is making it all wrong. Time. Everything. It's breaking up. If I stay here, I'll kill you. We'll all die!"

So, the words "I'll kill you" were a warning not a threat. Some comfort in that. And clearly Joe believed what he was saying. But did I?

Mona didn't. No way.

"We can't let you go, Joe," she said. "You're not well. Look at you."

His face was flushed, the skin starting to turn blotchy. His temperature so high, you could feel the heat from him.

"But what if it's true?" I asked Mona. "It could be. It all fits. The coins in his pocket. The things Nora told us about the rock. It could be the centre of some sort of time loop."

"Get real, Bug," said Mona. "Think about it. Think about what you're saying. Time slips, time travel, it's not possible. It won't ever be possible."

Part of me agreed. Part of me knew it wasn't possible but then neither was what I'd been through. What we'd both seen.

"It *could* be," I insisted. "People reckon that if you disturb time, everything goes freaky."

"I don't care how freaky it is," said Mona. "Whatever's going on, it's got nothing to do with time! Nobody can mess with time. Not now and certainly not in the 1950s or 1960s!"

"Well, someone did," said Joe. "Someone has!"

"What if it was someone from the future? Or some other dimension?" I said. "And they're using Demon's Rock as some sort of time portal?"

"It's a lump of rock, Bug," said Mona. "It's not a time portal any more than it's a crouching demon."

"Maybe the demon thing's connected," I said. "Maybe the people in the Middle Ages knew something odd was happening. And they explained it as magic and demons because that's all they understood."

"No," said Mona, shaking her head over and over.

"What then?" I asked, looking around the wrecked room. "How else do you explain all this?"

"I don't know," she said, sidling closer to me. "Some sort of mental illness. I've heard about stuff like that. People get so wound up, so disturbed, they can make things happen. Move stuff about without touching it. A bit like what you said before. A sort of mind control. Only they don't always know they're doing it."

"I'm not ill," said Joe. "Not like that. Not like you say. I was fine. I was all right. Till it happened. I'm not doing any of this. It's just happening, because I'm here. Now! Everything's breaking up. You have to believe me."

We were all so strung up that we jumped, all of us together, when the tinny music started to play. My mobile. Over by the seat. Where we'd left it.

Joe gawped as me and Mona headed for it. As though a singing bit of plastic was the oddest thing that had happened!

"Mum!" said Mona, as she picked up the mobile. "You've got to come home... House phone? No it's not engaged. It's broken. Never mind that. Listen to me! No, Mum, everything's not fine!"

"You better get back quick, Mum," I said, snatching the phone from Mona. "Oh, no! Mona! Stop him!"

Too late. Joe had disappeared out of the door, slamming it behind him. Seconds later I saw him race past the window.

"Of course I mean Joe," I shouted down the phone. "He's gone!"

Mum said to wait. Said she was just setting off. That she'd deal with it when she got back. But knowing what we knew, seeing what we'd seen, how could we wait? We couldn't just sit there doing nothing. We were both so hyped up it was physically impossible. We didn't stop to think. We just headed for the door without a clue what we were really doing.

We knew exactly where Joe was heading. It would be easy enough to catch up with him we told each other. Only he'd had a fair start and he was obviously faster and fitter than we were because, by the time we'd rounded the bend on the hill, there was no sign of him.

Possibly we'd have made better progress if we'd stopped talking or, rather, arguing with each other as we ran. Still totally confused.

About halfway up, I realized I was talking to myself. Mona wasn't with me. I turned to see her bending over, breathing heavily. I waited till she'd caught up before hurrying her on. The hill up to the moor is really steep and our original sprint had tired us out, so we struggled on at no more than a quick walk. At the top, the moor stretched out in front of us but we couldn't see Joe. Not too surprising because the moor isn't flat. It's full of dips and little rises, boulders, bushes and other things which interrupt the view, even on a clear day, which that Monday wasn't.

The rain had stopped but there was still a light, low-hanging mist. Nothing serious. Nothing threatening. Even so, Mona was reluctant to go any further.

"We ought to wait for Mum," she said. "She's sure to make her way up here."

"It'll be all right," I said. "We know where he is or where he's heading. It isn't too far. And we've got our phones if anything goes wrong."

Mona knows as well as I do that phones don't always work up there but she didn't argue.

"It'll be okay, it'll be okay," she muttered to herself as we headed towards the rock.

Coming from that direction, you don't see it immediately. You have to scramble down a slope and up the other side. Then you can't miss it. It's enormous. Or, at least it looks it, perched there on a fairly bleak and empty stretch of moor.

It certainly looked huge that day compared to the tiny figure beside it. We couldn't see what he was doing at first and we couldn't hear anything because the wind was rushing past our ears as we started to run. But as we got closer, we could see him, hammering, clawing at the rock. Hear him crying out.

"I've come back. I've come back. I want to go home. Let me go home."

It sounded so desperate, so sad, that Mona burst into tears and even I shuddered when I saw the state of Joe's hands. His nails ripped, his fingers bleeding from trying to tear into the rock.

"There's nothing there, Joe," said Mona, clutching him, hugging him, just like Mum would have done. "There's nothing there. It's just a rock."

Mona's words and a sudden gust of cold air brought me to my senses. She was right. It was a rock. A geological feature. Nothing more. It didn't look like a crouching demon and it certainly wasn't a time portal.

Joe was ill. Maybe I was ill. All that mattered now was getting back. Getting home. Only it wasn't that simple. And if what had happened at home was weird, what happened out on that moor was totally beyond belief. Something that turned my whole life upside down, inside out. So it will never be the same again. Not ever. Not as long as I live.

# Chapter Nine

The sky collapsed. That's the only way I can describe it. One minute we were standing in a hazy mist, the next we could see nothing at all. Not the rock. Not each other.

Probably we called out. Reached out. I'm not sure. Because accompanying the blackness was a huge roar like a hundred fighter jets flying low. The ground trembled and the rock started to glow, splitting the darkness. A still, red glow at first, which suddenly turned into a burst of fire. Swirling multicoloured flames, whirling in front of us like a tornado. Snatching us up. Spinning us around. Pulling, stretching, crushing, spinning, all at once, until I was sure that my body was going to be torn apart.

There was a sensation of falling too. At a speed I can barely describe. As if I'd leaped out of a plane without a parachute.

And pain. Pain like I'd never felt before. Burning, agonizing pain in my chest, my lungs, my limbs. A pain I was sure I could never survive.

Then, at some point, the pain stopped. Gave way to a floating feeling, as though there was a parachute after all. I must have had my eyes closed for a while because I remember opening them, seeing clouds of red dust shimmering around me, seeing Joe and Mona floating past. Even seeing myself. As if my mind were totally detached from my body.

And all the time I was telling myself it couldn't be real. None of it was real. It was hallucination. Sickness. It had to be. I could feel pressure building up again, in my head, behind my eyes, as if they were about to pop right out.

Did I lose consciousness? Probably. But for how long? Impossible to know. All I can be sure of is that when I came round I was lying face down on what felt like soft, dry sand. Listening to a rumble of thunder, seeing bursts of lightning hitting the ground not far from where I lay. Black powdery ground like fine soot.

Senses! I had senses. Sight. Hearing. Touch. So, alive then. Everything attached and in place. And no pain. Just breathlessness. So maybe, if I closed my eyes, screwed them up tight, opened them again slowly, all this would be gone. There'd be my bed. My room. Familiar scenes. Familiar faces.

"Bug, Bug! Get up. You have to get up."

Brilliant! It had worked. Mona's whining voice, rousing me from sleep.

"Bug, where arc we? What's happened?"

Not so good. Scrunch eyes shut again. Wait for it to pass.

"Bug, *please*. Wake up. You have to wake up."

Hands gripping each of my arms, pulling me to my feet. Two people holding me. One on either side. Mona on the right. Joe on the left. And, right in front of me, Demon's Rock. Battered, worn, eroded, with light bouncing from it, but Demon's Rock all the same. I was sure.

"Look," Joe shrieked, shaking my arm.

The pair of them pulled me away from the rock and swung me round, forcing me to see what they'd already seen. It was hard to take in, partly because I was having trouble breathing. And partly because Joe and Mona wouldn't let me stand still. They were constantly pushing, shoving, pulling, and dodging the streaks of lightning that speared down at us.

No natural lightning this, though. It was coming from enormous towers. Metallic. Shiny. Tall. Irregular. Like twisted pyramids glistening red. Seven of them. A long way off. Spaced at equal intervals. Circling the rock. And between them, instead of the moor, with its clumps of grass, bushes and scattered stones, there stretched only dry, black desert.

Words Joe had said earlier leaped into what was left of my mind. "Right place, wrong time." And all the time I was looking, trying to make sense of it all, Joe and Mona were pulling me round, pounding me with questions in hoarse whispers.

"Where are we?"

"What's happening?"

"Why can't I breathe properly?"

"There's something moving, Bug! In the towers. I can see them. What are they?"

Well, Mona's always had better eyesight than me and I guess I'd been too strung up to notice detail, but once she'd pointed it out, I tried to focus. Ignore the light. Look past it. Beyond it. To the towers.

What had seemed like shiny metal now appeared transparent, like glass. And Mona was right. Something, or someone, was moving about in there. Only it was impossible to say what or who. It wasn't just the distance and the blinding light. It was the speed.

The creatures, the things in the towers, were moving so quickly it was like watching a speeded-up video. Only even faster. Colours blurred, lines distorted.

People. They definitely looked like people. Red people. Long-limbed. Movement fluid. They seemed small, but maybe that was the distance.

"What are they? Bug, do something!"

What did Mona expect me to do? I'm not sure. There wasn't time to do anything. In the few seconds that my brain had been trying to process the information, a massive rolling wall, a tidal wave of orange-red light had opened up between two of the towers and was speeding towards us.

Maybe *that's* what Mona had wanted me to do. Stop it! As if! As if anyone could stop something like that. Already it was too late. The wave had smashed into us, passed through us, folded round us, become part of us, all at the same time. We were imprisoned in a cage of light and scorching heat.

No, not a cage. It was more like being in a vast tank of water. Only the water was light and the light was everywhere. Pressing in on us, shooting out sparks and flames. Flames and sparks that looked real, radiated real heat. But, like Joe had said, they didn't burn.

What I find hardest to explain is the speed at which all this happened. So fast that I'm sure some memories have been lost. In fact, I'm sure there were things going on that I didn't see at all. Things Mona remembers that I don't. Like the creatures.

All I know is that one minute we were alone. The three of us, huddled together, gibbering and shaking. And the next minute, we were surrounded. Mona swears they came out of the flames. She says they *were* the flames. Flames that suddenly started to take on shape, become solid, like us.

Maybe she's right. Where else could they have come from? Those creatures. Red, fast. Smaller, thinner than us. Dozens of them, with long limbs reaching out to grab us.

Impossible in the speed, the panic, to work out any features, but they had faces. And they spoke. I'm sure they spoke. Only the sound was high-pitched, squeaky, like a damaged tape. And I wish it had been a tape. So I could run it back. Replay it. Because I'd give anything now to know what they said.

But, at the time, I didn't care. Too terrified to watch or listen, all I could do was close my eyes and scream as they reached out and grabbed Joe, tearing him away from us.

Even with my eyes closed, I saw the flash, felt the blast. A blast that shot me forward like I'd been fired from a cannon. The sickening thud of my own body slamming into the ground, the snap of limbs breaking. Then silence.

Silence and darkness. Real or unreal? Conscious or unconscious? Drifting in and out of both. Reliving scenes over and over. In sequence. Out of sequence. Vaguely. Vividly. All mixed up.

Joe shivering in our doorway. The creatures snatching at us. Nutty Nora smiling her gummy smile. My mum pouring water into a hot-water bottle. Demon's Rock erupting. My dad rubbing cream into the scratches on his cheek. Joe again, with wild, burning eyes.

And, most vividly of all, the illness. A tiny virus nibbling its way through my brain, growing long, worm-like as it feeds on grey, spongy cells. Then fatter with huge, constricting muscles until it's sitting there, a gluttonous snake, coiled where my brain used to be. Mona's small white hands, reaching inside my head, trying to strangle the snake, unravel it, pull it out.

"Bug, Bug!" Her voice calling to me.

"Help me," I try to answer but no sound comes.

My body shaking. Being shaken. My eyes opening into darkness. Not total. Not blackness. Dark, but light enough to see Mona's shape. To sense the presence of the rock.

"Where am I?"

Stupid question but at least my voice was working. The question should have been when, though, not where. When am I?

Because, as I started to come round properly, to realize that my bones weren't broken and my brain was still working, I saw the towers. No light this time. No red moving figures. Just twisted shapes in the distance.

"He's gone!" Mona was shouting at me. "He's gone! They took him. They took Joe. And they left us here. Bug, they left us here! What are we going to do? What are we going to do?"

I stood up. Pressed myself against the rock for support, fighting down the waves of sickness, of emptiness. While we'd been snatched up in the light I'd been able to breathe, now I was struggling again, choking. As though the air was too thin or, even worse, poisonous.

"Is this real?" I gasped.

"Of course it's real," said Mona. "How could it not be real?"

"Hallucinations *seem* real," I said. "Remember Uncle Saul? When he was in hospital that time? Complaining about parrots flying around the ward?"

"Yeah, but he was on morphine," said Mona. "For the pain. The drugs caused the parrots and he was the only one who saw them! We've all seen this. You, me...Joe."

Her voice trailed and she looked round, hoping he'd appear.

"Maybe there never was a Joe," I said. "Maybe you're not even here. This is a dream, an illness..."

"You're not helping!" Mona yelled, bursting into tears. "You're not helping, Bug! You can't just pretend it isn't happening. Because it is. And I don't like it. I can't stand it. I want to go home."

She started to move but I pulled her back. Made her stand still. Made her look at me.

"You can't go home," I told her. "Not like that. You can't just run off home. Because if all this is real, home won't be there, will it?"

The crying gave way to coughing. But tears still poured from her eyes.

"Like Joe's home wasn't there?" she said.

I nodded. We stood there for a moment, watching, listening. And I don't think either of us liked what we saw, what we heard.

It wasn't only that the landscape was so bleak, so unfamiliar. It wasn't the mysterious towers or the unnatural silence. It was the whole atmosphere of the place. The time. There was no movement. No hint of a scurrying animal. No birds. Not even an insect flying past.

Apart from the towers, it was completely desolated, lifeless. I think that's what scared me more than anything. Finding yourself in some futuristic landscape was one thing. But an empty future? A dead future?

What had happened? What disaster had brought the moor to this? And was it just the moor? Or the whole country? The world? Were the creatures in the towers trying to put it right with some sort of time experiments? Or were the experiments themselves causing the chaos? Was this place, this scene, somehow existing out of time? In some other dimension?

"Where do you think Joe is?" Mona whispered, at last. "What do you think they've done to him?"

"Maybe he's gone home," I said, hopefully. "He seemed to think...didn't he...that they were going to send him back? To his own time."

"I don't know," said Mona, shuddering, looking towards one of the towers. "Whoever they are, whenever they are, whatever they're doing, I get the feeling...the feeling that they're not in control."

It was a feeling I'd had too but didn't want to admit it, even to myself. The creatures, the people, if that's what they were, hadn't seemed menacing. Not really. It's hard to say where the impression came from but we both felt it.

"We're not supposed to be here," Mona said. "They didn't mean to bring us here, to leave us here, I'm sure. We just got caught up in something..."

"It doesn't help though," I said, feeling the panic tightening my chest. "It doesn't help, does it? How are we going to get home? What can we do? We can't stay here."

"What if," said Mona, slowly, "we headed for one of the towers?"

Not a bad idea. And we might have done it, might have set off, if we hadn't been so paralysed with fear. Both of us too terrified to make the first move. Frozen there, waiting.

The first flicker of hope was exactly that. A flicker. Pale light from one of the towers. A few sparks and a rumble like a creaky old generator lurching into action.

"Something's happening," Mona breathed.

Something, yes. But what? And could you trust it? Did we have a choice?

As a second tower flared into life, my instincts changed. I didn't want to be there. Didn't want to be thrown, lurched, bounced around into some random time or place. Didn't want to feel the pain of my body, my mind, being broken up and thrown back together again. Didn't want to take the chance.

"Run," I shouted to Mona. "Run!"

# Chapter Ten

"**N**o!" screamed Mona, holding me back, her nails digging into my wrist. "I can't. I can't move. I can't breathe properly. There's nowhere to go. We have to stay. It's our only chance."

In the instant we hesitated, a wall of light opened up between the two flickering towers, just like before. Only before, it had sped towards us. This time it juddered and died. Opening an escape route again.

Except Mona was right. We couldn't escape, could we? Not on our own. We were in their hands. Their spindly, red hands and they'd failed us.

For a moment, their failure made me more angry than scared.

"Do something!" I tried to shout. "Do something! Don't leave us."

But the shout came out as a whisper. Something they couldn't possibly hear. Or could they?

Another burst of light. This time from a different tower. Stronger. More intense. Was this it? No. The light had to come from two towers, didn't it? Connecting together. But the other towers remained in darkness.

Whatever they were trying to do wasn't working. We were stranded. Out of time. Out of our minds. Out of our senses. Coughing. Choking. Too weak now to stand or even speak. We slumped down at the base of the rock. Watching the twisted towers.

Nothing. Then, suddenly, without warning, everything. All seven towers blazed into action at once. Releasing so much light, so much power, that I felt my body squeezing, compressing, spinning, even before it hit us. I never felt the contact. And I don't really remember what happened next. Except for this...

There's a dream I get now. A recurring dream. Of being an insect. A wasp, I think, sleepily crawling around in a carpet of dust. Being sucked up by a vacuum cleaner. Whipped up through a tube at an impossible speed, my soft body being battered and pulped against the sides. Down another tube, whirling in a drum of light, dust particles tumbling about. Trying to flap my ripped and battered wings, trying to break free.

Mona dreams of being an insect too. A butterfly. But she's trapped inside a firework, squashed, compressed in the powdery darkness. Exploding with it, as the touch paper's lit. And her wings are pulled from her, becoming the multicoloured sparks of the firework, she says. Shooting really high before finally burning up in the atmosphere.

Images, ideas of what it was like. Experiences locked in our subconscious. Feelings of being completely out of time, out of space. And when we finally start to connect with reality again, to see glimpses of familiar landscapes, we're light-headed, giggly. So it barely strikes us as strange that the fields, the outline of Demon's Rock, the houses and our village are all rushing towards us through a hazy, red mist.

Our house looms in front of us. But is it ours? Or has time moved on without us?

Relief as we find ourselves standing in our lounge. And yes, it is ours because the furniture's all there. Our parents are there. Sitting on the settee, watching TV, like nothing's happened. There's no mess. No sign of all the disturbance earlier.

We try to move towards them but we can't. We're held fast. We don't move.

They do. My parents. They both turn, as if aware of something. But they don't see us. We're not there. We think we are but we're not. But if we're not there, then where are we?

Is this death? An image, an imprint of ourselves? Some future scene, at home, where Mum and Dad have become resigned to our loss. Or have no memory of us at all?

That's when the sickness comes. Mona and me both feel it at roughly the same time. The nausea, the aching limbs. We feel our legs shake and a sharp pain hits us behind our eyes. A pain so intense that it forces our eyes shut and when we open them again, we've moved.

We're still seeing Mum and Dad. But this time at the kitchen table. They're looking at something. A document of some kind. Dad's tapping at a calculator.

"This payment here," Mum's saying. "What was that for? Oh, I know. It was Bug and Mona's new school jumpers."

Bank statement. They're checking their bank

statement. Mum's said that before. Those very words. Any minute now, she'll look up. Speak to us.

"Have you done that dishwasher yet?" she says.

But we don't follow the script. We both start shouting, rushing towards the table.

"What the heck?" says Dad. "Be careful! What do you mean, you're back?"

We know then that they don't remember and we do something really weird. Mona and me slip back into the conversation of Friday night, just before Joe arrived.

"I did it last night."

"No, you didn't."

We didn't want to but we couldn't help it. Couldn't stop ourselves going through the motions. But at the same time, we're staring, expectantly, at the door. Because whatever we say, whatever we do, we know it's not the same. Isn't ever going to be the same. We feel ill, for a start. Confused, weak. So disorientated, it's difficult to stand up.

We do though. We stand and we wait. But no one comes bursting in. And there's something else too. Something else is wrong. Mona knows it but she can't pinpoint it either.

"What are you doing now?" Mum said. "What are you waiting for?"

"Joe!" Mona yelled, breaking free from the pretence.

"Joe?" said Mum. "Who's Joe?"

"Joe!" said Mona. "Don't you remember? Joe! He comes in. He's supposed to come in. Now."

"Is this a game?" said Mum, knowing full well that Mona and me don't play make-believe. "Have you been making up a game?"

"What day is it?" I asked.

"Friday, like it's been all day," said Dad, his eyebrow raised.

"No, it hasn't!" Mona said. "That's where you're wrong. It started off as Monday. And Joe was here but then he escaped and we went after him and the rock exploded and now you say it's Friday again."

"Is this something you're working on for school?" said Mum. "A story?"

Then it hit me. The differences. The things that were wrong. Mum's plates. Mum's "broken" Italian plates were back on the dresser, where they'd always been. And the walls. The walls were wrong.

"When did you paint the walls?" I asked.

"Sorry?" said Mum, still looking quizzically at Mona.

"They're yellow," I said. "They're not supposed to be yellow."

"They're supposed to be white," said Mona, staring round the room. "Why aren't they white? Everything else is the same, isn't it, Bug? It's just the walls. Why should the walls be different?"

"I feel sick," I said, sinking down into a chair.

"What *have* you been doing?" said Mum, going over towards Mona, feeling her forehead. "You look flushed, the pair of you. And you're burning up."

"Early night, for both of you," said Dad. "And you'll feel fine again in the morning."

Fine. The word made me look up at his cheek and down at my own wrist. There were no scratches. No bite mark. How could there be? There'd never been a Joe, had there? Not in this time line.

Mona suddenly swayed and threw up all over Mum. And the sight of the vomit set me off, didn't it? So we're both there retching and puking, with Mum and Dad grabbing buckets, tutting about "something they've picked up at school".

Within an hour, they'd called the doctor because it wasn't only the sickness. Mona was complaining of a headache and lights behind her eyes while I'd come up in some horrible, blotchy rash.

The doctor said he was sure it wasn't meningitis but that he was going to admit us to hospital, just to be on the safe side. So an ambulance turned up at our house, just like it did on that other Friday. Only it wasn't Joe who was bustled into it. It was us.

Five days we spent in hospital. Five days of tests and examinations. The doctors were a bit baffled but, finally, they put it down to an allergic reaction!

Well, fine. I know allergic reactions can be pretty bad. Fatal in some cases. They can cause fever, hallucinations. But can they make two people imagine three days that never happened? Imagine the same thing in every detail? No way!

Mum and Dad were happy enough with the diagnosis, though, and Mona and me decided to play along. What else could we do? Every time we tried explaining about Joe, about what happened, Mum started to cry and the doctors just shoved some more pills down our throats. So we gave up, didn't we? But the minute we were allowed out we set off trying to track down what had really happened to us.

The obvious place to start was the rock. But we didn't. Partly because we were too terrified even to think of going back there. And partly because Mum wouldn't let us out for a couple of days anyway. She wanted to keep an eye on us, she said.

So we spent our time huddled at the computer, checking the Internet. Trying to confirm our theory that we'd travelled to the future and back again. The first thing we did was try to track down Joe. See if he existed. Whether he'd ever existed. We found loads of references to people with that name. Over 130,000! But however we refined our search none of them seemed to be our Joe.

It was the same when we drifted onto time-travel sites. There were hints and clues. Einstein's idea that time travellers would appear with a red glow...or the site claiming that large rocks could be the centre of space-time distorting energies. Not to mention the thousands of personal experiences. But none of them really proved anything.

And I was desperate for some proof because, as the days passed, something was happening to us. Our memories of those lost days were growing fainter. Fading much faster than "normal" memories. Doubts began to creep into our conversation. Could it have been sickness, hallucination after all?

That's why I started to write it all down. Determined to have something to hold on to. And I'm glad I did because just as Mona and me were really starting to doubt our own sanity, we found the evidence. The proof we'd been searching for.

All it took was a visit to Nora. Notice I don't call her Nutty Nora. Because she wasn't. Not any more. Sure, Nora was still frail. Still using her frame to propel herself about. But there was a brightness about her that hadn't been there before. Me and Mona both noticed the difference the minute we handed over the magazine Mum had sent.

Instead of staring at it in her usual vacant way, Nora started flicking through, commenting on celebrities and even making little jokes. Jokes that actually made sense! Spoken in brisk sentences. No rambling. No confusion. This wasn't just Nora having a "good" day. This was such a different Nora that, instead of making a quick escape, we accepted her offer of drinks and flopped down onto the settee.

"Is anything wrong?" Nora asked, as we sat there with our mouths drooping open. "Your mum said you'd been a bit poorly recently."

"Poorly?" Mona repeated. "I don't know. I'm not sure..."

"Miss Tamsworth," I said, certain I was on to something important. "We're doing this local history thing, at school. And I thought I'd try to find out about our house. You know...who lived there in the past and everything."

"We've got as far back as the sixties," Mona joined in. "And we think there was a family called Hadley living there. Is that right?"

"That's right, dear. Yes," Nora said.

She remembered them! She remembered the Hadleys. They really existed.

"Very nice family, they were," said Nora. "Had two lovely boys. Joe and Peter."

"And can you remember what they looked like?" I asked. "The boys?"

"Oh, I can do better than that," said Nora. "I have a photo of them somewhere. Now, let me think. Ah, yes. Pass me that blue album, dear."

Mona reached up to grab the album from the shelf. It was one we'd seen before. We've seen all of Nora's albums at one time or another but I swear we'd never seen this particular photo. The one Nora flicked to in the middle. Two lads grinning. A small one. And Joe. Slightly younger than when we met him, but definitely Joe.

"Then the family moved away..." I said, desperately trying to remember the details. "1966, I think."

"Yes, that would be about right," said Nora, sending a cold shudder right through me.

Our kitchen walls might have changed, Nora might have changed, dozens of other things might have changed, but the Hadley's hadn't. They'd left in 1966. Which could only mean one thing. We'd made it back from our time jump but poor Joe clearly hadn't.

"Mr. Hadley had a breakdown, didn't he?" Mona asked, hesitantly. "After his son went missing."

Confusion in Nora's eyes, reminding me, for a minute, of the old Nora.

"No," she said. "I don't know where you've got that from, love. Neither of his lads ever went missing, though they were both terrors for roaming. That Joe, especially. Used to scare me, he did. Riding off onto that moor on his own. Strange things have happened up there over the years, believe me, but no harm ever came to Joe Hadley. Or young Peter. Not that I know of."

"So why did they leave, then?" I asked. "Why did the Hadleys leave? What happened to them? Where did they go?"

"Bit of a funny story that," said Nora, slowly, as Mona and I waited. "Mr. Hadley made a bet. He'd never been a betting man, but Joe kept pestering him. To bet on the outcome of the next World Cup. And, as Joe had been quite poorly, I guess his dad decided to humour him."

"Poorly?" Mona said. "What kind of poorly?"

"Some sort of fever," said Nora. "Took him ages to recover properly. And even after that, he wasn't what you'd call strong. Didn't sleep well at night. Kept having nightmares and hallucinations. Said he saw the World Cup final in one of his dreams! Got his dad to bet on the finalists, the score, even one of the goal scorers, I seem to remember. Well, I wish I had dreams like that because, do you know, the lad was right!"

We did our best to look surprised.

"The bet was put on early," Nora said, "before the tournament even began, so they made a small fortune and used the money to buy a farm in Australia. They thought the climate might be better for Joe. Help him shake off the illness, properly. Get strong again."

"And did he?" I asked.

"Yes," said Nora. "He was fine. I kept in touch with the family for a while. Christmas cards, that sort of thing. But then it drifted to a stop...you know how things do...as time passes."

Time. Time passing in a nice straight line. Something I'd never questioned until our experiences at Demon's Rock. Now I barely know what to think. If people in the future are doing time experiments, as I believe they are, how can anyone be sure of anything? Scary thought that! So I try not to dwell on it too much. Especially late at night.

What I do think about a lot, though, is Joe. Does he remember any of his experiences? Did he write them down? Might he contact us one day?

We still haven't given up hope of finding *him* and we're still researching time-travel...though perhaps not quite so obsessively as we used to. And if we ever start to doubt again, all we have to do is read over our story. Remind ourselves of every crazy detail.

And yes, I know it does sound crazy but, like I said, every word is true. Somehow though, I doubt if you'll believe it...unless one day it happens to you.

# MORE CHILLING STORIES TO KEEP YOU AWAKE AT NIGHT

# USBORNE THRILLERS

## TERRY DEARY

### The Boy Who Haunted Himself

There's no escape from the ghost in his mind.

ISBN: 0 7460 6036 X

## MALCOLM ROSE

### The Tortured Wood

Who will be the next victim?

ISBN: 0 7460 6035 1

## ANN EVANS

### The Beast

How can you kill something that's already dead?

ISBN: 0 7460 6034 3

## PAUL STEWART

### The Curse of Magoria

Will anyone escape the deadly dance of time?

ISBN: 0 7460 6232 X

All books are priced at £4.99